Daniil
&
Vanya

MARIE-HÉLÈNE LAROCHELLE

translated by Michelle Winters

Daniil & Vanya

MARIE-HÉLÈNE LAROCHELLE

translated by Michelle Winters

Invisible Publishing
Halifax & Prince Edward County

Daniil et Vanya © Marie-Hélène Larochelle, 2017
Originally published in French by Éditions Québec Amérique
English translation © Michelle Winters, 2020

Library and Archives Canada Cataloguing in Publication

Title: Daniil and Vanya / Marie-Hélène Larochelle;
[translated by] Michelle Winters. Other titles: Daniil et Vanya. English

Names: Larochelle, Marie-Hélène, author.
        Winters, Michelle, 1972- translator.

Description: Translation of: Daniil et Vanya.

Identifiers: Canadiana (print) 20200285033
            Canadiana (ebook) 20200285084
            ISBN 9781988784571 (softcover)
            ISBN 9781988784618 (HTML)

Classification: LCC PS8623.A7615 D3613 2020 | DDC C843/.6—dc23

Cover and interior design by Megan Fildes | Typeset in Laurentian
With thanks to type designer Rod McDonald

Printed and bound in Canada

Invisible Publishing | Halifax & Prince Edward County
www.invisiblepublishing.com

Published with the generous assistance of the Canada Council for the Arts, the Ontario Arts Council, and the Government of Canada.

 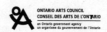

To defeat

CONTENT NOTES

These content notes are made available so readers can inform themselves; some readers may also consider these notes to be spoilers. This book includes references to unsuccessful pregnancy; toxic relationships; self-harm; and sadistic and sexual violence committed by major characters, which may include children.

PART ONE

GISELE LAID OUT THE EVALUATION FOLDER next to the cup of tea I made her and took out the first of the forms.

"It says here you have a cat," she began, checking a box.

Jules rubbed himself around her ankles, purring. He was a beautiful cat, surprisingly affectionate for a Siamese, and adored by all who met him.

"What will you do if the child is allergic?"

"Oh! We'd get rid of him, of course," I jumped in.

Gregory shot me a brutal look. He opened his mouth, but said nothing.

"So you'd abandon the cat," Gisele said.

I realized there was no good answer and had to back-pedal a little. "Well, I mean we'd find him another family, of course. Everybody loves Jules! Us most of all!"

I saw Gregory briefly close his eyes and run a hand slowly down his beard in a gesture of restraint. It was his cat, in all honesty, but I've always taken good care of him. I got up to add some water to the teapot. I wore slippers and set my feet down delicately to slow my steps. I took the time to listen to the water boil, my hands flat on the counter's cold granite.

Giselle and Gregory didn't speak as they waited for me to return. I poured the hot water on the leaves and watched the tannins gradually disperse. The trip to the kitchen and back gave me time to calm down a little. I'd been agonizing over this home psychosocial evaluation for days. We had already met with Giselle at the agency. She had presented us the adoption country options, the documents to complete, timelines, costs. The first meetings were very technical.

I worried today might not go as smoothly.

She'd never been especially friendly and was no more so in our home. As soon as I sat down, she explained to us that the interview would be carried out in two parts: first she would ask about our motivation to adopt and personal history, then she would conduct a home inspection. She had mentioned it when we set up the appointment and we were well prepared. We had, however, neglected to discuss the cat.

"So your marriage is solid, then? You're not trying to mend a crumbling relationship by adopting a child? Once the child arrives, will you change jobs? How does your family feel about the adoption? Your friends?"

Giselle wore a too-tight flowered top and black polyester pants that were developing pills. Jules rubbed persistently against her legs, covering her already lint-covered pants in blond fur. As she rhymed off questions, I stared at her blouse; it hung open at the neck, not quite revealing her brassiere, which I bet was beige. Gregory quickly stepped in to answer this time. With his elbows resting on his knees, he told her about his brother and his four children, his parents and mine, not mentioning that we didn't get along with any of them.

"Your last name, is that Polish?"

"Dominik. Yes, my father's grandparents immigrated to Quebec in the 1850s."

Gregory made a point of not telling her that he'd never set foot in Poland and instead reminded her that we'd left everything behind to merge our company with a friend's and were now firmly established in Toronto.

"We've created some work contracts at the firm that are very favourable for young families. We have an employee on maternity leave right now. Emma will be able to take advantage of the best work conditions," he joked, winking at me.

Giselle took notes without interrupting Gregory, watching my reaction.

"What's your reason for choosing international adoption?" She turned briskly toward me.

My voice started to quaver. I explained that I'd had a pregnancy medically terminated at twenty-eight weeks and the doctor advised against becoming pregnant again. It was almost true. I held her gaze for a moment as I listed the medical details. They had detected spina bifida in the fetus, I was supposed to have an abortion, but since the pregnancy was advanced, I gave birth to the baby, stillborn. A little boy.

In my cup, the tea leaves floated toward the surface before sinking to the bottom. The fine porcelain burned in my hands. Gregory broke the encroaching silence by talking about our beliefs, worldview, and social ethics. "There are so many children in need, and we have so much to offer!"

"Do you think of this as a humanitarian gesture to save a child, a charitable act to help an underdeveloped country?" she interrupted.

"Oh, we're like any other parents; we just want a baby."

His blue eyes landed knowingly on Giselle. She held back a smile. I shifted focus by saying that we had been together for close to ten years, that we had met in university, and that we'd always wanted children. Recounting it brought me back to Côte de la Fabrique, in Quebec. With our backs against the grey stone of the School of Architecture, smoking cigarettes, we had declared all our desires.

Neither of us had really smoked, but we'd used it as an excuse to meet up between classes. We were so young. We'd had the same will to excel, and had fallen in love with each other's ambition. As I spoke, I slipped a hand up the sleeve of my sweater, revealing my forearm. Gregory's expression suddenly changed and his lips tightened. I quickly covered back up.

It was hard to tell whether Giselle had noticed the exchange, as she was still taking notes. I crossed my legs and let my attention pass to the window behind her. Children were coming home from school, walking loudly down the snowy sidewalk. Their woollen hats bounced with their laughter. The snow melted beneath their steps into slushy mud.

"We live right by the elementary school, which will be a big help."

I had taken the time to think. Giselle approved with a subtle nod of her head and Gregory relaxed. She closed the first file folder, and then pushed back her plastic glasses, which had slid down her nose, and opened a second, thinner, folder. I could see rudimentary floor plans designed to be filled in.

We stood up calmly, imitating her movements.

"So you've seen the downstairs. Nothing to hide here, since everything is out in the open, as you can see," Gregory joked.

We lived in a traditional Edwardian house, but we had knocked down all the walls to make it feel more spacious. From the front door, you could see straight to the back wall of the kitchen. A central island separated it from the dining room. Nothing defined the boundaries of the living room except an Acapulco chair and a hide rug.

"You have a gas stove."

We were ready for this one.

"Yes, but look, we have the safety shield to block the knobs," I said proudly, pulling a long piece of metal out of the drawer.

"All right."

We led her upstairs and walked her from room to room, pointing out each of our creations.

"The shower is glass," she said, sliding the door.

"It's bulletproof, best you can get. Practically unbreakable. We recommend this one for families," Gregory assured her in his professional voice.

"The baby will get to use the bathtub first," I added.

"I've never seen a square bathtub before," Giselle said, visibly impressed.

"The upstairs was divided into four bedrooms when we bought the house, but we combined two of them last year to get some more space in the bathroom. Emma likes to get dolled up."

Gregory thought he was funny, and Giselle seemed to as well. She tucked a strand of hair behind her ear, stealing a look at herself in the mirror. I gestured for her to go first as we left the bathroom.

We had moved nearly everything out of my office to show how accommodating it was for more than one child. My drawing table sat forlornly in the big white room. Jules stood in the middle of the floor in a sunbeam. He let Giselle walk right around him without moving a whisker. She circled the room, looking at the bare floor and walls. She had taken her boots off when she arrived and was wearing thin nylon socks that revealed bright red polish on her toes.

As she walked into our bedroom, she stopped, mesmerized. Our clothes faced each other in an enormous walk-in closet that took up the entire back wall of our room.

"Emma designed it," said Gregory. He paused. Giselle's mouth hung open.

"Magnificent balance of wood and glass, isn't it? We've reproduced this dozens of times for our clients."

Giselle walked out of the room without taking any notes and distractedly adjusted her bangs. The upstairs tour ended in Gregory's office.

"What's that?" she said, pointing to the bookshelf with a distasteful look.

"Oh, uh, it's a mould of my teeth," said Gregory.

He'd had a mouthguard made last summer to whiten his teeth. When the dentist gave him the yellow plaster cast, we laughed about how hideous it was and Gregory decided to put it on display. His teeth were perfectly aligned, and were all the same size, even the canines. But the mould also contained the gums and ended in a flattened fleshy lump that made the teeth look especially morbid in a way that we found very funny. Giselle was not amused. She tilted her head, still contemplating the horrifying knick-knack.

"You can get a good view of the backyard from this window. Come see," I said, guiding her there with a hand on her shoulder. "I have some lovely rose bushes on the brick wall in the summer. That one's a cherry tree and the little one is a fig tree."

"You manage to grow figs in the city?" she said. "How?"

I launched into a long explanation of bush pruning methods, leading her down the stairs to the first floor and to the patio doors that opened onto the garden.

"It's too cold to go out, but as you can see we have an exceptionally large yard for Toronto. It's more than a hundred square metres. That's what convinced us to buy this house."

She didn't seem particularly impressed. She must have been from the suburbs.

"There's also the screening room in the basement," I said.

Giselle went down, holding onto the handrail. Jules snaked past her.

The basement was vast and empty. Gregory used a remote control to lower the projector screen.

Giselle took a few notes, eyebrows raised. "What's behind this door?" she asked.

"Over here is the laundry room and over there is another bathroom. Gregory's studio is at the very back."

She wanted to see everything, opening every cupboard. The cleaning products were all out of reach and the studio was protected by a latch set high on the door. Her interest started to wane. She stifled a yawn as she retraced her steps.

I politely helped her with her coat, following the movement of her shoulders. She pulled on her fake fur boots and promised she would contact us during the week to follow up.

She shook my hand limply and I closed the door. A gust of wind blew into the house as Giselle left. Still holding the doorknob, I turned and sighed at Gregory, sprawled on the couch. The house was calm again, and dusk was falling, casting a shadow like a blanket. I absently twisted my wedding ring on my finger, thinking back on the answers I'd given. Better replies were coming to me now that it was too late.

Gregory still said nothing, but patted his thighs to attract Jules as he crossed the living room.

"Honestly, you'd get rid of him just like that?"

BUT GISELLE DIDN'T GET BACK TO US DURING THE WEEK, like she'd said she would. I was sure we'd failed the interview. When she called me directly at the office three weeks later, I expected to have my worst fears confirmed.

"Emma, I have very good news," she said. "We've found an adoption candidate."

A hot wave spread through my stomach.

"In fact," she continued after a pause, "we've found two! Emma, a Saint Petersburg orphanage has a set of twins up for international adoption. They just confirmed it today."

I couldn't believe it. We'd done it. We were going to be parents. And it was Russia. The agency also had connections in China and South Africa, but we'd stated our preference. We were going to have everything we wanted. And twins! I started to shake. I caught my breath and dialed Gregory's number, even though his office was just on the other side of the wall.

When he opened the door a few seconds later, the glass door sprang on its hinges. I stood up suddenly, too fast, and my eyes went blurry; I had to steady myself on my drawing table to get my balance.

"Two babies. Do you know how lucky we are? Twins! Twins!" That's all I could say.

Gregory was also caught up in the details. "Are they identical?" he asked.

"I didn't know; she didn't say."

"What do we have to do now?" asked Gregory quickly, seized by doubt.

"We have to go sign the papers, tonight if possible."

"Let's go—right now!"

We left the office that minute. Our family name was spelled out in capital letters on the door that closed behind us.

Giselle passed me the photo of the boys with a measured hand. The black-and-white portraits were taken head-on. A number had been hand-written on the bottom border. The lighting was strange; their faces were overexposed compared with the completely black background, giving their features a reform-school look. I turned the images lovingly toward Gregory.

"They're magnificent."

They had thin faces with fleshy mouths, and their shaved hair was very blond. They didn't smile, focusing sternly on the camera. An uncanny resemblance united them. It was like I was touching them for the first time. I caressed the glossy paper with my fingertips.

"My babies..."

My shoulders started to shake. Could it possibly work this time? I started to sob and Gregory took me in his arms. With my nose in his shirt, I calmed down, just breathing him in. The fabric was soft and warm, and underneath it, his chest beat forcefully. I was going to be a mother.

Giselle resumed her explanation. "They're fifteen months. They've just arrived at the orphanage. You're first on the list, but you have to move fast."

She paused. I got the feeling she wasn't finished.

"There are still a number of papers to sign, and you'll need a visa to enter the country, but we'll expect you to be in Russia before the weekend."

It was happening so fast. I thought of work, of maternity leave, of the clients we'd have to notify at the last minute, of the upheaval this would create at the office, of packing, of the house that wasn't ready.

"The circumstances of this adoption are unique," Giselle stressed. We couldn't go as a group, like it was usually done. We had to go alone. The timelines were too tight. The agency couldn't even free up a staff member to accompany us. "Will you be able to manage?" she asked.

We were ready to make every promise, to agree to everything required. We signed the papers hastily, already in a celebratory mood.

WE ARRIVED IN RUSSIA, exhausted before we had even begun the adoption. We'd rushed our preparations: I'd handed off my files to a colleague, tried to ready the house, and thrown some things in a bag. We'd bought our plane tickets at the last minute, which cost a fortune.

Despite the fatigue, I hadn't managed to sleep on the plane, and only relaxed as we were about to land. I staggered off the plane holding Gregory's arm. My body demanded a real night's sleep. I wasn't used to travelling in these conditions. It was unbearable.

Getting through customs took an eternity. I was too hot in my Isabel Marant down jacket and I was worried about the bags we hadn't picked up yet; if we took too long, they could get lost or stolen. After we repeatedly explained the nature of our trip, one customs officer finally understood and called to a second, who led us into an isolated room to prolong the interrogation. They made us wait a long time. Gregory dozed off, one elbow on the table. My eyes itched and my mouth was dry.

The room was in terrible shape. The floor tiles were encrusted with dirt and the bare walls emanated the smell of sweaty bodies. Several bag straps cut into my shoulders, but I didn't dare set anything on the ground. The fluorescent lights reminded me of a Blockbuster Video store.

Two agents finally came in. With their brushcuts and sunken, mean expressions, they looked very much alike in their stiff uniforms, even if one appeared slightly younger. The older one rested his hand on the brown folder before him. He spoke first, in a rough French. "Are there not," he asked, "children to adopt in your own country?"

His eyes creased and he seemed to vomit the words. Gregory fixed him with a confident eye. It wasn't a real question; they weren't expecting a real response.

"You can't make them yourselves," the other said to him sarcastically.

They were trying to provoke him, but Gregory wouldn't take the bait. The younger one undressed me with his eyes. It was disgusting. I started scratching the polish off my nails. The other one finally opened the folder, licking his finger to turn the pages.

"We're not familiar with your agency. Who have you been dealing with in Russia?"

"Here," said Gregory, pulling out the papers. The older one took the document and slid it under his pile without breaking eye contact with Gregory. I focused on the pointed letters of his nametag, unable to read his name. The older one was shuffling the pages of our folder. He wasn't really reading, but his movements implied there was a problem. With a tilt of his chin, he signalled to his companion to join him in the corner of the room. They knew we didn't understand Russian. I held my breath. Did they have the power to ruin this?

Then I guessed what awaited us. They returned and sat down, their chairs screeching against the dirty floor. The young one lowered his chin, in order to look up at us. "You haven't paid the adoption tax," he said.

Obviously.

He rolled the customs stamp in his hand. His fingers were short and square. He might as well have put his dick on the table.

Gregory shifted to sit at the very edge of his seat and leaned forward as if preparing for an attack. He looked directly at the young customs agent. They sized each other up for a moment, blinking. Then Gregory suddenly placed his wallet on the table and slid it toward the man, keeping his hand on top. He then firmly sat back and crossed his arms, a defiant smile on his lips.

The two Russians eyed each other. The younger one opened the wallet and quickly counted the wad of cash inside. Gregory must have had two or three hundred euros, maybe five. The young customs agent pocketed all of it, and the other stamped the document that released us.

We walked out, heads held high, without saying a word.

We took a taxi to our hotel. Tired but too restless to sleep, we stretched out on the bed's rough sheets. I was still for a moment, studying the cramped room. Every inch was in use, down to the tiny sink in the corner that would clearly overflow. The double bed faced the door and two small cutouts in the headboard served as night tables. To the right was a closet that smelled of raw wood, and facing us was a desk with a straight-backed chair.

When Gregory went to wash up, he discovered that the shower head only came to his shoulders and the toilet was too close to the door to comfortably sit. "Great," he said. "I'm going to have to poop with the door open."

We laughed together for a moment, which roused me.

He plugged in his laptop. His clients, unlike mine, hadn't even been notified of his absence. He was sure he could easily make them overlook the delay. He was working on a kitchen design. I stretched, yawning. I wanted to look at the orphanage's website, even though we knew the site by heart after visiting it dozens of times. The garden, the cafeteria, the dormitories, the games room, the inside courtyard and the swing set: it had all become familiar. When Gregory opened the page, the connection was too slow and no pictures would load.

"Do you want to get something to eat?"

We were exhausted, but it was too early to go to bed. We had to resist and get ourselves on Russian time. We had chosen the hotel for its proximity to the orphanage, even if it was far from the tourist area. In any case, we weren't there as tourists. We decided to take the streetcar to the city centre. The hotel clerk directed us to a stop nearby and we set off on foot. It was cool out, but I was still too hot in my winter coat. I had only packed warm clothes, expecting Saint Petersburg to be much colder than Toronto. Every time I pictured Russia, it was covered in snow and ice. It turned out, strangely, to be fairly warm.

The streetcar stop looked like a train station: there were multiple tracks, two in either direction, separating a central platform. A number of people were waiting, smoking. I watched their faces, looking for distinctive features, ones I might recognize tomorrow in my sons. I decided that close-set, deep eyes and short foreheads seemed typically Russian. Otherwise, the station occupants were not dressed very differently from Torontonians, and nothing on the platform made me feel out of place. When our streetcar arrived, I was surprised to discover that the red and white vehicles looked a lot like the ones we have in Toronto. I can't say why, but I felt suddenly disappointed.

The route was a straight line and we struggled to stay awake, rocked by the movement of the car. My thoughts became fuzzy. Pressed up against Gregory, I rested my head on his shoulder. When he moved, I could feel his muscles sharpen powerfully. The nape of his neck was downy with salt and pepper hair that blended into his beard. His neck was nearly as wide as his head. In comparison, I looked very fragile. I noticed few Russians with beards.

As soon as we stepped down, the coolness of the city helped keep us awake. We lazily followed the canals leading to the Church of the Savior on Spilled Blood. To the left was an enormous concrete building, punctured with red-brick-bordered windows. We walked down a side street overhung with decorative arches. I sensed Gregory was elsewhere. He wasn't at all focused on our walk. Neither was I. We said nothing, wandering without paying attention to this city we were discovering for the first time; this outing seemed to me a tedious preamble to the important part.

On the other side of the canal, the cathedral revealed itself. The sight of it shocked us out of our reverie. Gigantic, its square base stretched out in towers topped with numerous pointed domes in blue or gold, some sculpted with a spiral pattern. The first half of the building was dominated by triangular forms, softening the second half, which was all elegant curves. Colourful mosaics decorated the entire surface of the cathedral, textured spectacularly with delicate reliefs. Gregory hugged me. We were fascinated. Here, the sky was stunningly clear. From our oblique point of view, we could see tourists huddled around the main façade.

"Shall we go in?" asked Gregory, kissing me on the cheek.

"No," I said. "I'm good here."

I was hypnotized by the magnitude of human effort. This splendour was part of our children's heritage.

Our children!

We still hadn't reached a consensus on names. Gregory told me I was being superstitious. My baby had had a name, and I never got to say it. I didn't want to rush the decision.

The twins already had Russian names, but Gregory wanted to choose new, more North American ones. He didn't want the boys to feel marginalized; moreover, the names had to be bilingual, which limited our choices. We'd drawn up lists of names, none of which were right. But very naturally, standing in front of this magnificent cathedral, the issue was resolved.

"I want them to keep their names," I said.

There was no discussion of my decision. They were named Daniil and Vanya. We would meet them tomorrow.

That night, we jumped on each other, pausing only to kiss and absorb each other's moans. Gregory took his time rolling my clitoris between two fingers, waiting as I shuddered, and penetrated me in one brisk, almost violent thrust. Our ragged breath dictated the rhythm. And, very soon, the sheets were saturated with our sharp, pungent sweat.

I WOKE UP IN THE MIDDLE OF THE NIGHT, unable to get back to sleep. The hotel room seemed suddenly unwelcoming. The mattress, which was too hard, resisted my movements and the sheets had a chemical smell. The hot air from the ventilation system was blowing directly at me. I turned, groaning, toward Gregory, but the covers formed a shell around him.

The clothes I'd picked out for the meeting were laid out on the chair before me: a pair of slim pants, a top with embroidery around the neckline, and a pair of Frye boots, more comfortable and stable than heels for carrying children. I planned to bring my Herschel bag for the visit. I hadn't bought cumbersome gifts, just a stuffed animal for each— a blue striped cat and a green monkey, also striped, in knit cotton—and a few organic cotton outfits. I played the scene of our meeting on a loop in my head, trying to imagine their smiles, and perhaps their tears. My stomach was in anxious knots; I was suddenly afraid I'd caught some bug.

I was already showered and dressed when Gregory emerged from the blankets. I sat on the bed and put a hand on his waist. He grabbed it and pulled me to him.

"Stop!" I said. "You're going to mess me up."

"Hey now, come on," he said.

He pretended to undress me and I escaped, half genuinely upset. Hands on hips, I told him to hurry up and get ready. I couldn't stand still anymore. We needed to get out of here. The room was suffocating me. I was already at the door, tensed like a runner at the starting block.

It was less than ten minutes' walk to the orphanage. The cold air did me the most good. I still felt feverish, but less nervous. Gregory had opened a Google Map and I had brought a tourist guide, even though the route was straight and clear. I don't know how we still managed to get lost. We ended up in an abandoned alleyway, with graffiti painted in contrasting layers of colour. Stencils, tags, and English obscenities were scrawled alongside metal structures and rusted pipes. Despite the filth, there was a certain aesthetic to the arrangement. I pulled out my phone and took a few pictures.

Piles of wet clothes and cardboard littered the ground. Grey snow sat heaped against the walls. Suddenly, a pile of garbage stirred. I jumped, grasping Gregory's arm. He froze, moving me behind him protectively as a little brown head emerged.

It was a child.

He scanned us with vacant eyes before trying to stand. He was wearing an old man's hat with earflaps and a threadbare down parka. Strands of greasy hair stuck to his forehead. Very shaky on his legs, he sat right back down and rummaged in his clutter for a plastic bag, which he placed over his mouth and nose. At first I thought he was hyperventilating, before I realized he was sniffing glue. He couldn't have been more than ten years old. His fingers, black with grime at the knuckles, were still plump.

I glanced at Gregory. He caught me by the elbow and dragged me quickly toward the main street, feeling it necessary to add, "We can't save them all." I agreed with a nod.

We passed through a poor suburban residential neighbourhood. All the houses and buildings were built of cinder blocks, the windows were in terrible shape, and the curtains did nothing to hide the poverty. A damp moss clung to the visible power lines entangled over our heads and ran in brown patches on the walls. The image clashed with the luminous palaces and canals pictured on the front of my guide book, but didn't surprise me.

The two-lane road we walked up was filled with European cars: Škoda, Renault, Volkswagen, Citroën. On the sidewalk, people looked at their feet as they made their way to work. A woman with flat, yellow hair walked ahead of us. She was young, but her shoulders were stooped under her jean jacket. She stopped to talk to a round-headed man with gelled hair; her thin lips were painted in too-pink lipstick.

The sun couldn't break through the layer of clouds. The crust of snow on the ground was black and icy, and we had to walk carefully to keep from slipping.

"There it is."

Low and rectangular, the structure looked like a school, but something was off. There were several grated windows on the upper floor, but none on the ground one. The roof looked to be little more than a flimsy layer of crumbling shingles. Around one side, we could make out a dirt yard in which sat a neglected swing set.

We fell silent. The ice squeaked under our steps. An oily smell permeated the dry, cold air. Discarded plastic and dead grass mingled in a patch of snow. I didn't recognize the place; nothing looked like the website.

We climbed the steps as though walking into a church. As we announced ourselves on the intercom, I was seized with emotion.

The director greeted us with a firm handshake and let her eyes linger on me. She didn't look me in the eye, but stared instead at the tinted glasses on top of my head. We sat patiently on peeling leather armchairs as she reviewed our adoption folder. She was ageless, her face a plaster mask of makeup. She wore a white wraparound dress with a tag pinned to her chest, on which her name was written in pink: Vonda. The dress was very low-cut and Gregory couldn't stop ogling her chest. I took out a tube of hand cream to occupy myself while I waited.

"Everything looks fine," she announced in a crisp French. "You can take the children when you come back tomorrow."

Gregory asked her to repeat herself, and she confirmed we could sign the release forms the next day. We'd expected a number of short visits in the days to come. It was an essential adjustment period; it could take over two weeks to complete the process, Giselle had advised us. I'd bought open-ended plane tickets for this reason. Vonda didn't register our surprise and rose briskly, giving us an artificial smile. She led us through the corridors of the orphanage without really bothering to show us around.

The smell of bleach was suffocating. Craning our necks here and there, we tried to get a feel for the labyrinth of the place. The hallway opened onto different-sized rooms. I thought I saw a TV room, cluttered with wheelchairs. We passed a dormitory lined with the beds of older residents. The dormitory for the little ones was farther on, crowded with dozens of numbered metal cribs. We took the main staircase upstairs. Several children sat on the steps. A damp little hand grabbed mine. The child smiled at me through creased eyes. He wouldn't let go of my hand. Vonda pushed him back, and, on seeing my expression, explained with a wave of her hand, "These ones are vegetables. There's no hope for them."

An uneasy feeling overtook me. What was this place?

The second story had two extra dormitories, for severely disabled children. The rooms were crammed with beds with retractable bars, and various pulley and support systems. Even the hallways were overcrowded. A soundtrack of cries and moans accompanied our passage. Vonda quickly walked us past a bathroom containing a clump of towels and children slopping in puddles.

Green dominated the decor. An indefinable green. Watery green. Dirty green. Drowning green.

I clung to Gregory's arm. Even he was a little unstable.

The door to the playroom opened with a slam. A racket escaped from within, freezing us for a moment on the threshold. A single barred window lit the room. Low bookshelves and white melamine furniture covered nearly all the walls, containing few books or toys. But that all disappeared once the director pointed to the left-hand corner of the room.

There they were!

I was paralyzed for a moment with vertigo. My breath sped up and the ground beneath my feet went soft.

I had made it.

With tears in my eyes, I hid a smile behind my hand; I had to catch my breath before taking a few uncertain steps toward them.

They were watching the activity in the room. I got down on my knees to bring myself to their height. Gregory pulled up his pant legs and bent down as well. His hands shook a little.

The boys looked at us, perfectly still, and blinked slowly. My cheeks were wet with tears and my nose had started to run. I pulled a tissue out of my bag, laughing, finally relaxed.

"Vanya?" I guessed.

Although he didn't respond, I knew I was right. I turned to his brother.

"Hello, Daniil," I said.

But he also remained there, slack-armed. Their hands were clean, their nails cut short. Their big blue eyes were fixed on us, passing from Gregory to me without batting an eyelid. They didn't smile. Their cheeks were pink with mild eczema. Both wore T-shirts and light grey shorts. Their resemblance was striking.

The noise level was hard to endure. Dozens of children were shrieking at the same time and no one was trying to console them. The twins were not crying, but neither were they overjoyed at our presence. Seated side by side and straight-backed, they seemed interested in nothing in particular. They were waiting patiently for something, we didn't know what. They seemed fine just to be there, together. They weren't touching, but something in their attitude, in their posture, formed a unit. Around us, foam balls landed, stuffed animals were shaken, puzzle pieces scattered—the room held only soft, safe toys. Clearly, they wanted to keep the children from hurting themselves. The loudest were ten or twelve years old. In the centre of the room, fifteen babies, all dressed in the same grey uniform, were crowded into a big enclosure with wooden bars.

As the morning went on, we quickly learned to tell the boys apart. Daniil was fair skinned, his eyebrows and eyelashes so pale they were practically invisible. With a wet pout, Vanya observed the world inquisitively. While more frail than his brother, he was also more mobile. After heading off on his hands and knees, he took a few steps back towards us. One of his feet turned inward; he didn't so much limp as hop from one foot to the other.

The babies eventually let us pick them up. I pulled my hair back in a loose chignon, a natural gesture to keep it out of the way. Soft and plump, Daniil smelled like damp biscuits. When I brought my face close to his, I noticed a scar starting at his brow bone. It must have been a serious wound, as there were stripes still visible on his forehead, even though you could see it had healed. I stroked it with my finger, as if to erase it. Vanya was more fragile. His little joints were bony. He exuded a lemony, vegetable scent. I inhaled the hollow of their necks for a long time. I didn't know what else to do other than cuddle them. It was hard to get their attention and they didn't want to play. They didn't understand French, and we didn't speak Russian. We had to appreciate just being there with them.

Gregory's beard intrigued Daniil; he reached out his hand and touched it with his fingertip, which made Gregory laugh. Holding each of them in turn, he patted the contours of their bodies, trying to resist squeezing them too hard. They had muscular calves and straight shoulders. They were big, healthy boys. Gregory was visibly filled with an immense pride and was already in love with them.

When I got out my phone to take some photos, an employee rushed to let me know it was forbidden. She didn't speak French, but her abrupt tone was unequivocal.

The director appeared again to let us know it was time to leave. We had a very hard time separating ourselves from the babies, even though they showed no emotion as they watched us retreat. I kissed them each on the forehead, whispering, "Mommy will be right back. Mommy will get you out of this place."

Vonda walked so fast we nearly had to run to keep up with her. She hadn't authorized us to stay for lunch. She didn't think the bag I'd handed her would be useful, and told me to bring it the next day for their discharge. When we asked her for more details, she shrugged and replied that releasing the children was simply a formality.

Pushed to the exit, we found ourselves once again on the street a few moments later, before I could understand what was happening. I looked back as the door closed behind us, stripping me of my children. The feeling of being ejected and evacuated from my own life reawakened all my buried anguish.

THEY PUT ME ON AN OPERATING TABLE, in case there were complications with the delivery. Two nurses and a doctor busied themselves around me. They had been with me all day, but I didn't want to remember their names or faces. They were vague shadows I refused to identify. I looked only at Gregory so as not to see their movements. A furrow split his brow. He squeezed my hand between his.

Instruments clicked on metal trays. Nurses forcefully massaged my stomach and their hands rummaged inside me. My name echoed throughout the room, but I was unable to respond. They were emptying me out. The epidural had numbed me, so I only experienced the pressure, the agitation. The smell of iodine caught in my throat. I felt a final suction and then my feet were soaking wet. I let go of Gregory's hand. My fingers scrambled over my forehead, my eyes, my mouth; I was drowning.

Gregory wept into my hair.

A nurse wrapped the baby in a blanket and handed it to me sadly. She paused. Her voice was soft. She guided my movements for me to take it. My body convulsed with sobs and contractions. I was afraid I would drop it, my hands were shaking so badly. His face was waxy, his stunted limbs glistened. His delicate skin seemed to contain water rather than organs. I wasn't ready to see him this way. I looked at him, my eyes clouded with tears, the poor little bundle in the crook of my elbow. His bottom was pointed, protruding under the blanket; no one had bothered to diaper him. I rocked him, saying his name over and over, my mouth distorted.

An aroma of uncooked bread dough, of yeast, rose from him. I plunged my nose into his neck. I wanted to lick him, to absorb him, but they were already taking him away.

My son was going to have an autopsy.

I howled, clinging to Gregory's neck, digging my nails into his back, drenching him with tears and snot. A horrible migraine was swelling in my skull, making me dizzy with pain. The walls shifted before my eyes.

Curled up in the sterile bed, I didn't sit up when a nurse came in, harshly announcing herself. She pressed the electric bed's control button. A few palpations assured her my uterus had regained a normal shape. Under the hospital gown, I could feel my sagging belly, swollen as if it still carried a baby. I turned my head to bury my face again in the pillow.

I didn't know where Gregory was. They may have told me.

As the nurse exited the room, I mumbled that I needed to use the bathroom. She helped me out of bed, then promptly left. Staggering in pain, I dragged the IV pole behind me and sat down on the toilet. They had put an enormous disposable diaper on me. My stomach folded softly over the elastic. The saturated medical pad fell on the floor, covering it with patches of lumpy blood. Folded in two, my chest against my thighs, I waited out a contraction. The burning made me retch. I tossed the soiled tissue, but didn't have the strength to wipe up the mess. Blood had started to dry on my ankles.

Before leaving the bathroom, I caught a look at myself in the mirror. My lips, eyes, and hair seemed scrambled, their colours washed out.

I resumed my position in the bed and slid under the messy sheets, damp with tears and sweat. They had given me a private room, vast and bright. Behind the closed door, I heard the cries of newborns. Their screams distorted as a pain pulsed in my temples. There was no bassinet in my room. Only silence, in the room as in my belly, devoid of life.

I thought back to the moment they injected the baby with morphine. Gregory stood at my side, determined to shoulder the decision for both of us. He held my hand firmly, already resigned. A long needle passed through my belly button, to reach the baby directly. Then I held out my arm, offering up my veins. The tube went in, and the nurse massaged the saline bag to make sure the liquid was flowing smoothly. With her hand on my shoulder, she assured me this would only take a few minutes. These precautions were repulsive. I wished they would stomp on my belly or beat me black and blue, rather than try to ease my suffering.

I was sure I could feel the moment his heart stopped. I imagined him floating in my stomach, moving his little toes, his little fingers... and then suddenly, no more. Eternally still. Hot saliva filled my mouth. I vomited a few streams of sour bile in the wastebasket.

My hair stuck to my forehead with sweat. I shivered. The suffering wasn't enough. I should have been the one to die on that operating table. Tears stung my cheeks. I threw my head back and gouged my nails into the flesh of my left arm, leaving a long, deep, three-pronged scrape. From my wrist to my elbow, the skin rolled up beneath my fingernails. I finally fell asleep.

When I woke, a young nurse was getting ready to bandage my arm. Her black hair was tied back in a neat ponytail. Her eyeshadow was meticulously applied. Her uniform was too tight to flatter her full figure.

"You shouldn't do that," she said.

She disinfected the wound.

"But don't worry," she added, smiling conspiratorially, "I didn't record it in your file. You can still be released this afternoon."

I pulled down the sleeve of my hospital gown to cover the bandage she'd just finished applying.

"Where is my husband?" I asked.

"I don't know, ma'am. I'm just starting my shift."

Her ponytail swayed across her back as she left. I scanned the room for my phone. It was a modern room, freshly renovated. The cupboards were fake mahogany; the colour matched the maroon curtains. My phone was not on the plastic tray next to me, and I didn't see it on the bedside table. Then I noticed my clothes folded on the grey leather armchair, and my purse. My phone would be inside. Over the chair hung a framed black-and-white photo of a mother feeding her baby. I clenched my teeth and lifted myself out of bed.

The spot on my hand where the IV had been was swollen with a big bruise. It was painful to work my phone. There were a number of texts from Gregory, and I had missed several calls, two of them from my friend Magalie, and one from my mother. I didn't read or listen to any of them, just texted Gregory. I didn't feel like talking.

"Come. I'm getting out."

I felt the device vibrating as I put it back in my bag, but I didn't answer.

SIX WEEKS LATER, I had to go through a standard postpartum exam. In my gynecologist's waiting room, I tried not to meet anyone's eyes. The happiness emanating from all the pregnant women was unbearable. It was like I could feel their pregnancy simply from the joyful satisfaction of their voices, the way they wriggled in their seats. They all wanted to talk, to exchange experiences, to compare bellies. A few weeks earlier, I'd have been excited about my appointment too.

"Emma?"

Dr. Maxwell closed the door to the exam room behind her. She spared me the meaningless "How are you?" and immediately opened my folder. "I know it's hard, Emma," she said.

The autopsy confirmed the ultrasound and amniocentesis. The fetus couldn't have survived. A silence fell between us. She was waiting for me to question her, but I had nothing left to say.

The gynecological exam was quick: manual exam, pap smear.

As I tucked my shirt back into my pants, she presented me with a number of pamphlets, one of which was for international adoption. She told me again that I was in perfect health, but that right now I was emotionally fragile. I was still young, nothing was stopping me from getting pregnant again, but it was up to me to determine whether I could handle it.

It was out of the question. I didn't want another child. That was the one I wanted. She told me that my reaction was entirely normal, and suggested that I take my time and talk to my husband about it. I slipped the brochures into my bag without responding.

"Feel free to contact me if there are any problems."

I called Gregory on my way to the elevator.

"I can't have any more children," I said.

"Oh Emma," he said, "we can talk about it later, okay? Do you want me to come get you?"

"No, that's okay," I said. "I have to go meet Magalie at Mercatto."

"Are you sure you're okay?"

"Yes," I said. "It was just a routine exam."

As I hurried across University Avenue, I glanced back through the corner of my eye at Mount Sinai, looming like a bunker. The air had suddenly grown chilly. A few weeks earlier, Toronto was in the midst of a heat wave; now everything seemed ready to die to make way for autumn. I was underdressed and shivered as I made my way to the restaurant. My discomfort seemed appropriate, just like the cramps that had run through my kidneys since the labour. The pain was reassuring, matching my state of mind.

Magalie stood up abruptly when she saw me through the front window of Mercatto. She was as dark as I was blond, as bright as I was pale. And yet, we were often mistaken for sisters. We had, it's true, the same slender frame, the same triangular face.

Since moving to Toronto, we'd established a whole new circle of friends. It largely revolved around Gregory, but Magalie was the exception. She wasn't in design; she was the administrative assistant at a French immersion school.

I met her because her boyfriend at the time was an intern at our office. We became friends primarily because she spoke French. She'd since married a software architect, and they had a one-year-old son.

The hostess at Mercatto smiled warmly at me when she saw my belly. I still looked about six months pregnant. Magalie shot her a dirty look, and hurried to take my arm as she led me to the table, like I was an old lady.

"Emma! How are you?"

I sighed and tried to come up with a response that would please her. I felt empty. Alone. Such clichés. The truth was that I wanted to torture myself, to punish myself. I wanted to destroy the body that had failed to give me a baby; to cut open my useless belly, plunge my hands into my innards and devour my own guilty uterus, the way mothers eat their own placentas. As far as I was concerned, my system was dead.

That was not the picture Magalie wanted me to paint.

For her sake, I forced a sad smile and said that it would get better, that I was happy she was there. As I spoke, I fingered the scars on my arm.

"I know you think I don't understand, but it's not true," she said. "You have the right not to be okay. You have the right to not want to talk about it, to not want to put yourself back there. Your pain is what's left of him."

My son, my pain. She understood after all.

In the following weeks, I thought often of that conversation with Magalie. It took me a long time to allow myself the right to feel better. Then one night, Gregory came home from work and I was sitting in the living room, petting the cat. He put down his bag in the entryway and came to join me. With his hand on my knee, he asked how my day had been.

"I dismantled the nursery," I said.

He pulled his hand back.

"I gave everything away."

Gregory gave his hair a nervous tousle. "To whom?" he asked.

"To the Salvation Army," I said.

The Egg cradle, the Stokke dresser, the Surya rug. Thousands of dollars spent at Ella + Elliot. He briefly opened his mouth and ran his tongue along his teeth.

"And you feel better?" he said.

"Yes. Much," I said confidently. "Also, I've decided we're going to demolish the room. I want to expand the bathroom."

TODAY WAS THE DAY. I was becoming a mother. In a few hours, Daniil and Vanya would be my sons. They existed. They were real. There was no risk of them disappearing. I could already see us, Gregory and me, leaving the orphanage with our boys in their brand-new stroller. Our twins, who would fly home with us to Canada. Today.

I was just doing the latches on the suitcases, putting our things in impeccable order. The speed of events no longer worried me. I'd made my peace and adjusted. I felt strong. Two children were now counting on me. I moved gracefully through the room, shoulders straight, hips forward, paying special attention to my posture. I mustn't forget anything. Gregory had arranged for the hotel to let us store our bags at reception while we went to pick up the children, and the taxi had been ordered. We would circle back for our bags, then go straight to the airport. It was a tight schedule, but our planning seemed flawless.

Gregory enjoyed assembling the double stroller, joking about the complexity of the design.

"Honestly," he said, "it would have been easier just to carry them in our arms for such a short distance."

But I wanted them to be comfortable, preparing for the possibility that they might not want us to carry them in our arms. They didn't really know us, after all.

Its wheels pristine, the stroller rolled for the first time down the streets of Saint Petersburg. A fine rain refused to fall, hanging instead in a thick fog. I pulled down the visors so the seats wouldn't get wet and closed the flaps of my trench coat. When we arrived, a group of children were playing in the muddy courtyard. They scratched at the layer of sandy snow, climbing on the structure of the swing set. Excited by our arrival, the pack pressed themselves against the chain-link fence, waving and shouting joyfully in their clipped tones.

Neither the director nor her assistant was there. An employee, Irina, seated us in the office. She handed me a yellow and blue BIC pen and a form and began pointing out the pages for us to sign, one at a time, passing the single pen back and forth. Gregory handed her the document. She detached the last page, stamped it, and handed it to us before inviting us to follow her.

The doors were closed and there were no children in the hallways. The place seemed deserted. The silence amplified the sound of our footsteps on the tiles. The corridor felt narrower than the day before. Irina led us to the twins' dormitory.

They were alone in the room. All the other beds were empty, and the covers had been folded into squares. Their metal cribs had been placed side by side. They slept curled up on their stomachs. Their bottoms, rounded by their diapers, lifted to the rhythm of their breath. "They're good sleepers," she said.

"Shouldn't we wait until they wake up?" I whispered. She assured me it wasn't necessary, and seemed in a hurry for us to get moving.

Gregory delicately lifted Vanya and placed him in the stroller's top seat. He buckled the seatbelt hesitantly, but the child sighed and stretched his legs without protest. In my arms, Daniil was warm and pliable. He started sucking his thumb when I set him in the bottom seat.

The employee admired the stroller.

"It's a Phil & Teds," I said.

And so the adoption was concluded.

She waved at us from the top of the stairs once we reached the sidewalk. Her young face was devoid of all emotion.

The babies woke up in the taxi. I calmly offered them a snack and wiped their mouths assuredly.

"You're a natural," raved the driver in astonishingly good English.

Gregory approved, his eyes misty.

As we entered the airport, I realized I hadn't paid any attention to it on our arrival, knocked out from the flight and the customs interrogation. The hall's triangular lines formed golden diamonds over our heads. The purity of the angles was dazzling. I felt luminous. While I lost myself in the ceiling design, Gregory folded the stroller, checked the car seats, and lugged the heavy bags with the pride of a patriarch.

The babies were going to spend many hours on our knees on the plane. Locating a sparse play area not far from our gate, I suggested we let them play for a while to stretch their legs before the flight.

Facing the wooden abacus, rotating puzzles, and slide, they clung to each other. I sat down on the foam rug and reached out my arms for them to join me. They took a few uncertain steps in my direction.

"Are they twins?" asked an enthusiastic young mother, who was accompanied by a young girl. She spoke French without an accent.

I proudly confirmed.

"They look just like you," she said. "How old are they?"

I froze. Should I correct her? "Fifteen months," I declared breathlessly.

It seemed fair not to mention the adoption; I wasn't about to tell my life story to a stranger. I turned my back to end the conversation and focused on the children.

The little girl babbled, jumping from one toy to the next. The twins had no reaction at all.

Suddenly, Vanya fell on his behind. Gregory lifted him to his feet, teasing him gently, before he noticed he was trembling.

"Let's get to the gate," he declared.

I put a sweater on Vanya, but the trembling didn't stop. I buried my nose in his neck and murmured over and over, "It's okay. Mommy's here."

I let the word *Mommy* roll around my mouth.

I held Vanya on my lap on the plane. He was getting worse. He cried violently as a fever gripped him. His little body boiled in my arms. I pulled off the sweater, not knowing whether I should warm him up or cool him down. I tried rocking him and singing gently to him, but nothing would calm him. He was having muscle spasms. I didn't know how to soothe him.

Then Daniil started to shiver as well.

"Maybe it's just a bad cold," ventured Gregory.

The seats were narrow and we didn't have much room to lay them down. I was getting warm myself and was fighting the start of a migraine. When I unbuckled my seat belt, I was able to reach the air vent overhead. A thin jet of air blew at us. Holding Daniil against him, Gregory got up and rocked him, standing in the aisle, but he kept having to squeeze against the seats to let the other passengers by. Daniil cried even harder.

A liquid spread through his pants. Daniil had diarrhea and his diaper was overflowing. I had brought a few changes of clothes for the babies, but of course, none for us. Gregory made his way to the bathroom to try and clean up the mess, leaving me alone with the two children. Vanya screamed in my lap while Daniil writhed on Gregory's seat. I raised the armrest separating us, trying to pull Daniil closer to keep him from falling on the floor. I shot panicked looks toward the bathrooms, hoping Gregory would hurry up and return. The babies were howling and people were starting to turn and look at us. I tried unsuccessfully to console them by making the stuffed monkey and cat talk. Gregory had alerted a flight attendant, who followed him to our seats with juice and blankets. The babies refused to drink. To get the plastic cup out of the way, I finished Vanya's juice myself.

I just couldn't believe a cold would put the children in this state, and the fact that they'd fallen sick at the same time suggested something more serious. I didn't understand. I watched Vanya's features, trying to discern the origin of the problem, but I realized I had no point of reference for a sick child. He wasn't coughing, his nose wasn't running, it didn't look like a cold at all, but I couldn't think what else it could possibly be. An infectious disease, maybe? I lifted his shirt to see if there was any redness or spots, but I saw nothing.

Next to me, on Gregory, Daniil started convulsing. We frantically hit the button for the flight attendant.

"Hurry, lay him out on the seat. Keep his airways open. Like this," she said.

She lifted Daniil's chin to stretch his trachea. I looked from one of them to the other. I monitored Vanya's condition as he struggled in my arms.

"What's wrong with him?" I said.

"I don't know, ma'am," she said. "We'll try and find a doctor. My colleague is moving passengers so that we can put you in the back."

I thanked her and discreetly turned my head to wipe my nose on my sleeve. With my cheek glued against Vanya's, I cried desperately along with him. We laid the babies out on two seats. The attendants found a doctor on the flight list. He briefly examined the boys, but only had a basic kit with him, and was reluctant to give a prognosis.

"I want to be absolutely sure of my diagnosis. I would need to get blood tests..." he said. "But these look to me like withdrawal symptoms."

"Withdrawal! What do you mean?"

"I would say—and I can't be completely sure—that they're manifesting symptoms of alcohol poisoning. Have you given them anything?"

"Of course not!" exclaimed Gregory.

"What I mean is, have you given them any cough syrup? Antihistamines?" he said. "If the child is allergic, there can be a reaction like this."

"No, no," replied Gregory, "We didn't give them anything."

"Has this ever happened before?" he asked.

We had to admit that we had just adopted the babies, and only met them the day before.

A silence fell over the scene.

Sick and lost amid a crowd of strangers, the babies howled hysterically, at the top of their lungs. It was hard to keep them on the seats. We had to hold them down firmly to keep them from falling off. Seeing our distress, the doctor tried to comfort us.

"You know, this condition isn't permanent. You have some long days ahead of you, but they'll recover. Don't worry."

Before that, his tone had been cold and professional. He was on vacation and could have done without an emergency consultation. He looked us over as he spoke. I felt horribly guilty. He hastened to add that there was nothing he could do for the children, that only time could heal them, and that the best thing to do would be to consult a pediatrician as soon as we got home. He removed himself quickly and returned to his seat.

The babies grew more and more aggressive as the hours went on. We had to contain their contortions and kicking, endure their biting and scratching.

"You have to secure them for landing," the flight attendant advised us.

A torture. Immobilized in Gregory's powerful arms, Daniil vomited his rage in furious hiccups.

THEY REMAINED UNDER OBSERVATION at SickKids Hospital for twenty-four hours, rehydrated intravenously. Nothing was going as planned. I found myself alone in an empty house. I sat hopelessly at the kitchen table, an oppressive silence all around me.

What had I imagined would happen? That becoming a parent would be like the glossy photos in the magazines?

I started thinking about my baby. Throughout the whole pregnancy, I'd watched what I ate, hadn't touched caffeine or alcohol, took a variety of vitamins, went swimming, did yoga, took naps, all for nothing. All my plans failed; even this adoption couldn't go normally. With my head in my hands, elbows on the table, I felt exhausted, wondering if we'd made the wrong decision.

A thought struck me: I lost the baby in August, more than a year and a half ago, and the twins were born in October, at nearly the very time my baby would have been due. I would have been pregnant at the same time as the Russian woman who had given birth to the twins. Who was she? Was she too young? Too poor? I wondered what she had eaten during her pregnancy, whether she'd taken drugs. I had done everything in my power to have a perfect pregnancy and created an unviable baby, while she, who may have done every single thing wrong, had given birth to healthy children she didn't want, who'd then been mistreated by an orphanage. This line of thinking led me nowhere.

Outside, the temperature was still glacial. Our electric thermometre showed 2.4 degrees Celsius. I knew because I had been staring at it, motionless, for at least twenty minutes. The heat came on in the house. A gust of warm air blew up from the vent behind me. I could feel my mouth and eyes drying up. With my eyelids closed, I moved my tongue around my mouth, but it made no difference. It felt like my whole body was scorched and rasping. The fabric of my clothes suddenly began to itch in a way my nails couldn't soothe. I scratched compulsively, as though a parasite was crawling under my skin. The more I scratched, the more the itch spread. My legs, arms, and then my hair prickled. Flakes of skin soon covered my shoulders. I swept them away briskly. My neck and arms were streaked with bright red, but the irritation was constant. I rolled up my pant leg to rub my calf, wanting to soothe every part of my body, but no comfort came. I tried to steady myself, taking deep breaths, my hands flat on the table to stop myself from scratching. The effort was unbearable. Tears clouded my eyes. I rummaged through the drawers and armed myself with a butter knife. Gripping the utensil with both hands, I rubbed the blade against the nape of my neck until a fresh wave of pain appeased me.

A deep calm now fell over the house. Gregory wasn't home. He had to stop by the office and would come home soon to pick me up and take me to the hospital to see the children. My breathing returned to normal and my mouth settled into a smile. I let my eyelids drift halfway shut and daydreamed. The babies would soon be through their withdrawal and everything would be better. After all, they weren't sick; we just needed to help them through their addiction and then everything could start for real. I had to be strong. For them.

I still had a little time before Gregory would be home, so I thought I'd make a cup of tea. When I stood up to go boil the water, I realized that I still had the butter knife in my hand. A hunk of bloody hair hung from the blade.

I quickly lifted a hand to the back of my neck and realized that I had an open wound. Blond hair stuck to my fingers. In a panic, I pressed a dishtowel to my wound, washed the knife, and went upstairs to change my top.

There was a lot of blood, but the cut wasn't deep. After cleaning it, I hid it easily under a little bandage. Shamefully holding the towel and my bloody clothes, I buried them at the bottom of the diaper pail.

Before going to the hospital, Gregory informed me that we were going to stop by the adoption agency. He had managed to get an emergency appointment, and the sooner we went, the better. We needed to get the situation cleared up.

"You want to return them?" asked Giselle violently. "Send them back to Russia?"

That obviously wasn't the issue. We simply wanted to understand: Why had they poisoned our children?

"There's nothing we can do," she said. "There's no legal recourse internationally. And then, what, do you want to shut down the orphanage? You don't know what the conditions are over there. They're doing what they can with what they have. And if you only knew—it's no better here. I don't know what world you're living in!"

Giselle's lack of understanding was baffling.

Her face contorted with rage. "You have two beautiful children. All you have to do is help them through this one little challenge. That's what responsible parents do."

Her chastising tone made my stomach contract in pain. She might have been right. Was I in the middle of failing my first maternal duty?

Gregory saw things differently, and lost control. "It's your agency we're going to close down. It's you we're going to sue!"

"Sir, having children always involves risk. They're not luxury items that come with a guarantee. You want to return them because they don't meet your standards? I can open a file and put them right back up for adoption. There are plenty of other families out there just waiting for a chance like this."

"Are you a complete idiot? It's not the children who are the problem, it's the whole shitty system that hasn't taken care of them! Your agency is working with criminal institutions!"

Giselle stood up in such a fury that her chair fell over backwards. "You have no right to speak to me that way!" she said. "I'm calling security—get out of my office. I'm the one who can revoke your custody of the children!"

Gregory stood and glared at her before catching my arm for me to follow him. "Come on," he said. "We're leaving!"

We sat for a moment in the parked car, speechless. Gregory gripped the wheel as though he was about to plow straight into the concrete wall ahead of us. I stared at the toes of my pumps without seeing them.

"We were tricked," I said, my voice breaking. I didn't know what tone to use.

Gregory, however, remained furious. "What do you want me to say?" he said. "That I chose the wrong agency? That I should have done something in Russia while there was still time? You want me to tell you this is all my fault? Okay, Emma, it's all my fault. Are you happy?"

"How could we not have noticed anything?"

"It all went so fast. I had so many things on my mind at the same time: the procedures, the interviews, the meetings. It was too much."

"You make it sound like I made you do everything. I was the one who planned the trip, bought the tickets, made the reservations, shopped, packed. What? You think you're the only one who cared?"

"I didn't say that. But ever since you lost the baby you've been so fragile, it's like you're going to fall apart any second. I feel like I have to handle everything."

"I never asked you to be my caretaker. I don't need you!"

"That's exactly the problem! How do you expect to build a family? All by yourself?"

"What family? We're nothing yet—they're not even..."

Gregory furrowed his brow. "They're not even what, Emma? What?"

I thought of their sweet faces as a sob muffled my words. Poor babies, as if on top of it all they needed their parents tearing each other apart. "Oh, Gregory... Let's go get them, okay? They're all alone at the hospital. Let's start doing it right. They're so worth it."

Gregory's fury melted away. He sighed, and a moment passed. "You're right," he said. "There's no sense fighting against what happened. They're all that matters now."

We were never going to set foot in that agency again. I didn't know if Giselle's threat was real, I didn't know if she actually had the power to revoke our custody of the babies, but I certainly wasn't about to test her. The very thought of being separated from my sons now made me shiver with horror. I promised myself that from now on, I would devote myself completely to them.

THE BOYS WERE RELEASED FROM THE HOSPITAL that same day. It turned out that there was no trace of alcohol left in their system by the time they were admitted. The nurses felt it was enough to treat them for dehydration. "You can get tests done at a private clinic, but as far as we're concerned, they're in perfect health." They suggested it may have been an allergic reaction, or lactose or gluten intolerance. They didn't know. We would just have to be vigilant. We could finally go home together. All together.

The twins tottered through the first floor of the house, checking out the space. The cat, intrigued, followed them everywhere. Daniil took to him right away and immediately nestled his head into Jules's fur, as blond as his own hair, delighting in the ticklish softness. Jules purred joyfully. When Vanya tried to climb onto the grey fabric chaise, Gregory helped him up. But at his touch, Vanya was startled and curled away protectively, terrified.

"It's okay, little man. You're home now. Daddy just wanted to help you."

The language barrier made contact difficult. We touched them gently as we spoke to them, in an exaggerated mime, so they could understand the meaning of our words. I had a sudden idea.

"Would you boys like to take a nice bubble bath?"

I took both of them by the hand to follow me upstairs. Gregory suggested he would make dinner in the meantime. We slowly climbed the stairs. I mimicked their steps, setting both feet on each stair. Jules snaked through our legs and waited for us at the top. "He's a naughty kitty, isn't he?"

The hint of a smile lit up their faces. I realized Jules was my key to winning them over. I thought briefly of the interview with Giselle, where I'd made the foolish mistake of suggesting we'd get rid of him. Poor Jules.

"Come on, boys. The bathroom is right here. You can help me run the bath." I placed my hand over Vanya's so he could help me turn the taps. Then I did the same with Daniil to pour the soap into the stream of water. The bathroom was soon filled with the smell of orange blossom and Mustela soap. Once I had adjusted the water temperature, I gently dipped them into the water one at a time. They acquiesced without a peep. As I soaped them, I got to tenderly discover their delicate bodies. Their skin was amazingly pale; not a single birthmark or freckle marred its perfect texture. In comparison with their unblemished flesh, my own skin seemed well-worn. I handled them like fragile, precious objects that at any moment could break apart.

I let them play in the water for a good half hour. They were perfectly calm and didn't splash at all. The hospital had warned us their behaviour might still be altered by their withdrawal over the next few weeks, and stressed that they might be irritable or angry. For the moment, they seemed timid and reserved, but I was ready for anything. One after the other, I dried them with a fluffy towel and warmed them against my chest. Their thick hair brushed against my face as I inhaled their fragrance. I didn't care for their military-style haircuts and vowed to let their beautiful blond hair grow out.

IT TOOK ME SEVERAL WEEKS before I would accept visitors. I suspected an unbearable voyeurism in the desire to meet the twins. But Gregory insisted.

Since the babies had arrived, I had gradually been increasing my safety perimeter around the house. For a while, the prolonged winter gave me a pretext for staying indoors. In the first weeks, I was overwhelmed with panic whenever I would go more than a kilometre from the house. I was afraid the babies would cry, afraid they'd get sick, afraid they'd throw a fit. I was constantly thinking back to the plane ride. I was terrified of reliving those moments, even though, for the time being, they were adapting well. At home, safe from prying eyes, I felt better. Gregory went back to work right away and fell back into his routine. He was impatient for me to bring the babies by the office to introduce them to our colleagues, a prospect that didn't excite me at all.

On Gregory's recommendation, I started by inviting Magalie over. Her son was now three, and he could become a good friend for the boys, but I was deeply apprehensive about this playdate. I hadn't officially introduced them to anyone. Our respective parents were supposed to be come and meet them, but they didn't seem to be in any more of a hurry about it than I was. Moreover, they all lived far away, which gave everyone a good excuse. I wondered if they'd have been more insistent if the twins were their biological grandchildren. My mother took the loss of my baby very hard and often asked when I would try again to get pregnant. When she understood that I didn't want to try again, she resumed her life. We sent photos regularly and talked on the phone. That was enough.

The morning of our playdate, I left the babies in just their diapers so that they wouldn't soil their clothes, dressing them at the last minute. I hesitated at the dresser for a long time before finally choosing two little sailor outfits. Magalie was scheduled to come over before their nap; the twins were easiest in the morning.

When I opened the door, Magalie stood in the middle of a mess of bags, in the midst of which was her son, Trevor. She had brought gifts for me, but also a number of items she no longer needed. I grinned fixedly as I watched her drag the clutter into the front hall. Sitting against the armchair in the living room, the twins watched this intrusion with a patient curiosity.

"They're beautiful!" she said.

She seemed surprised. What had she been imagining?

"It's crazy, they look like you—same light eyes, same hair, same skin tone..."

She had intended it as a compliment. But beneath the innocence of the remark, I could sense all her prejudices. Because my children were blond like me, it was a perfect deception. I had nothing to worry about, no one would be the wiser. I looked like their real mother, was that it? I suddenly hated her.

She moved toward them with such exaggerated playfulness that Vanya, frightened, kicked a foot in the air.

"You'll have to sign him up for tae kwon do," she tried to joke.

Magalie's husband was Korean. They lived in a semi-detached house north of Bloor Street in Little Korea. Trevor had inherited his father's eyes and his mother's light brown hair. Today, he was wearing a bright, sporty T-shirt, lightcoloured pants, and sneakers that lit up with every step. He approached the boys. They were all the same size, even though Magalie's son was nearly two years older. I peered at them proudly.

Trevor made a move toward the boys, and Vanya responded by clawing the air.

"Careful, honey!" said Magalie, petrified, as if my son was a wild beast.

"It's okay," I said defensively. "He didn't even touch him."

There was a sense of discomfort in the room that the cake we shared next couldn't allay. We tried talking as we normally did, but nothing was like before—or was I the only one who felt the difference? When I'd lost the baby, Trevor was just over a year old. When we would see each other, Magalie almost never brought him, out of sensitivity perhaps, or to ensure he didn't interrupt our conversations. I realized I hadn't seen her very often in her role as a mother, and I had just been thrust into my own with children who were no longer infants, yet I was expected to already know them. Magalie moved confidently, clearly had a routine, spoke to her son—who responded. So many little details showed that she was his mother. Meanwhile, my boys didn't look at me when I spoke, and didn't understand simple instructions, which made me look awkward. The juxtaposition was unbearable.

Before she left, Magalie wanted to go over how to use the items she'd brought me. I had to hide my disdain for her bargain, Disney-coloured hand-me-downs. Did she really understand me so little? Didn't she see that they didn't belong in my home? I thanked her as politely as I could and we hugged, promising to see each other soon.

As I closed the door, I laughed, picturing Gregory's reaction to this stuff. Our house was decorated with a rigorous consistency that had been acclaimed by a number of Toronto magazines. I considered sardonically that Magalie's shabby gifts might put the brakes on my husband's desire for socializing and I might just get a little peace.

WE DECIDED RIGHT AWAY to extend my maternity leave until the boys started school. The firm easily replaced me; there was no shortage of design interns in Toronto. I was still a partner as far as research went, and my office was waiting for me. Gregory promised that it was just a matter of time. He wanted me to stay at home with the children. He thought it was for the best, considering the circumstances. His argument was circular; he refused to place the boys in a traditional daycare structure. It would be like sending them back to the orphanage. He trusted no one, not even me.

And so I reorganized my life around them. I didn't really miss work, and had so many new preoccupations that I wasn't sure I'd have been able to focus on my clients' projects. Renovating a bathroom or organizing a wardrobe now seemed meaningless to me when compared with my sons' language instruction and social integration and establishing trust between us. In the past few months, they had become less timid, but still had trouble expressing themselves, which frustrated them. They were easily angered and impossible to console. When one of them was angry, it was his brother he turned to, never me. They often clung to each other, curled up together in the corners. At first, I found this cute, but over time, the gesture struck me as a brazen rejection.

The more time passed, the more it seemed to me that they understood what I was saying, but refused to listen. I even went so far as to translate a few words of Russian to be sure they were making the connection. "No/не", "come/ просто," "there/там," "here/здесь." It wasn't too complicated, but they pretended not to hear.

Every day was a steady stream of activities. The boys always woke early, around five-thirty. I tried to make them play quietly until Gregory woke up around seven. We ate breakfast together, and then, when Gregory left for work, I would spend a few hours at the neighbouring school's park to let them frolic before the other children arrived. Spring came, and while it was still grey outside, we could play for a little longer outside each day.

The days passed identically. I sat in the sandbox, making castles they wasted no time in stomping. When they ignored the reassuring hand I offered to them as they climbed a ladder or slid down the slide, I didn't let it bother me. Instead, I admired their courage and independence.

When the park filled up, we had to leave. The presence of other children overexcited them and they didn't know how to interact. They pushed, punched, and threw sand in order to get attention. I wondered if it was this kind of behaviour that the orphanage had tried to counteract with the alcohol. The other mothers seemed concerned when we were there. I hated them all.

The backyard then became our refuge. From the kitchen window, Jules, who was not allowed outdoors, oversaw our games. I sang them songs, threw the ball, created obstacle courses for them to run. I did everything I could to channel their energy. Inside the house, the twins misappropriated every toy within reach: cars became projectiles, building blocks were hurled against the walls, books torn, crayons devoured. Violence was part of the routine, but their conflicts particularly affected me. As an only child, I had a hard time understanding their aggression, never having fought with anyone at all. Gregory assured me it was normal for boys to play rough and reminded me that he and his brother used to fight all the time.

But I wasn't going to stop trying to break their violent habits. I devoted extra attention to their diet, and forbade them artificial colouring, gluten, sugar substitutes, and most processed foods that might lead to behavioural issues. I spent my evenings preparing special meals just for them.

Gregory would return from work each day to find me completely wiped out. He couldn't understand it. He thought I was on vacation.

"It's your turn to change a diaper." There was a hiss in my voice.

"You don't think maybe you should try and get them washed instead?"

The quarrels got more and more frequent. Gregory spent very little time with the boys, but he had no problem imposing his ideas, while not even taking the time to read the articles on modern parenting I recommended.

When we got loud, Vanya and Daniil stood stock-still, watching the spectacle intently, as though they didn't want to miss anything. The boys observed our behaviour with an interest they didn't lend to a single other educational activity.

"We're setting a bad example for them," said Gregory. "We really need to tone it down."

He was right. I tried my best to regain my composure.

"Mommy isn't angry with you," I said, trying to reassure them, opening up the arms where they would never take refuge.

Gregory told me I was doing too much. He wanted me to relax, and suggested that I spend an evening out. I was becoming wild, like the boys, he said. If I cut ties with all our friends, how were they supposed to learn to socialize?

He promised he'd participate more, and I promised to try and loosen up.

"Do you want to ask your mother to come visit?" he asked. "She could help out if you're finding it's too much work."

"No," I said. "I'm all right."

"Or mine?" he said. "She'd be happy to come and meet them. She was a big help to Ian when his girls were little."

I hadn't spent much time with my nieces, but the rare times I saw them, they called me Aunt Emma and had been excessively polite. The twins were nothing of the sort, and I could already hear my mother-in-law's comments.

"Listen, I'm fine. I don't need any help. I—"

He interrupted me. "What if we went camping?"

"Camping?" I said. "In the woods?"

"Of course," he said. "Come on, we'll do it right. I promise, we'll go glamping."

Gregory was kidding; he loved the outdoors, and had no need of the creature comforts I did. Just thinking about the preparations exhausted me, but he had made his decision and was already planning to take Friday off.

On Thursday I ran a few errands with the boys, then took advantage of their naptime to pack up our gear. I had to limit myself to a very small selection, as we would be going by canoe with very little room for provisions. It was only mid-May, but it was hot. I planned to bring summer clothes. There was already so much camping equipment that I only brought a few toys and the boys' stuffed animals. They would find plenty to entertain them in the woods. When I was done, six waterproof bags sat lined up on the bed. They were big, folding carriers that closed with a buckle. We had bought them several years ago, when we still lived in Quebec and regularly went on canoe trips—which is to say, a lifetime ago.

I had hoped to take grand trips through Europe or the States with the twins, but since the horror of our first flight, I wasn't eager to repeat the experience anytime soon. It was probably better to start off with something simple.

The hours in the car were difficult. The boys, it turned out, got motion sickness in the car, which meant we had to make a number of stops, considerably prolonging the drive. Fortunately, they loved the trip across Lake Muskoka. The weather was perfect and a gentle breeze ruffled their hair. Ours was the only boat on the water, so we had the lake all to ourselves. Wrapped up in their lifejackets, Daniil and Vanya leaned out to trail their fingers in the water, smiling serenely.

Gregory steered the canoe with ease. Nestled between his legs, I kept an eye on the boys up front. I felt happy, and let him do all the paddling, since he didn't really need me. This hadn't been a bad idea after all. The wilderness would do us all a world of good. The water lapped gently against the hull of the canoe, and the muddy smell of the lake was exhilarating.

The campsite Gregory had chosen was completely isolated on a rocky shore. A fully equipped yurt waited for us. I was surprised how comfortable it was: there was a living room with a little fireplace, three beds, and a kitchen. As soon as we arrived, we decided to unpack and start a fire. Gregory wanted to involve the boys. The three of them left for a long while, and returned with their arms loaded with firewood. The fire fascinated them. I realized that they may never have seen one before. Once we were all settled in, we let them play.

I'd bought a pair of rubber-soled canvas water shoes for each of us from the Walmart in the Dufferin Mall. They were hideous, but good for walking on the rocks and dried quickly. I'd been surprised to find that, while they were the same height, the boys had different shoe sizes; in their thin canvas sneakers, Daniil's feet were clearly a size larger than Vanya's. Gregory put his on and started waddling like a duck to make the boys laugh. They hesitated for a moment before following suit, walking behind him.

"Come on, let's put our feet together and get a picture of all our matching shoes."

We all pointed in a right toe and made a star. I took a picture underwater, which, with an Instagram filter, looked quite good. I remembered having similar sandals for playing in the water when I was young. My parents had never taken me camping, but we'd often gone to the beach in Maine. I remember being bored, playing alone in the waves. It was nice to know the boys would have each other to play with.

The water was shallow a long way out and the forest was sparse; I could let the boys explore, watching them from a distance. They seemed excited about the freedom and spent the afternoon digging in the rocks and clay with little bits of wood. I settled in at the edge of the lake in my Muskoka chair, rubbing lavender-scented cream into my hands. Next to me, Gregory read on his iPhone. The lake was grey, breaking in calm ripples on the shore. The pine trees stood in backlit silhouette on all sides of the lake, and in the distance, the hills rolled gently back the way we had come. Overhead, the geese honked, flying way up high. I watched them for a long time, my mind empty.

For dinner, we were breaking the rules with hot dogs and roasted marshmallows. Gregory gave each of the boys a long stick: "You're doing the cooking tonight." he said.

The boys looked at him blankly. Gregory showed them how to thread the hot dog on the stick to grill it. They caught on quickly and scarfed their meal like I'd never seen them do. Their faces sticky with ketchup and burnt sugar, the boys were radiant.

"Look, a beetle!" said Gregory suddenly.

The beetle had a big, black shell with a blue sheen. Its head and legs were lost in the pine needles that carpeted the ground. Gregory put his hand out flat and let it crawl slowly into his palm.

"You can touch him gently," he said. "His back is hard, to protect him from predators."

The twins barely glanced at the creature crawling toward Gregory's wrist. Transferring it to his other hand, he then set the bug down on a stone, since the boys didn't seem interested. The beetle stood still, shaking his antennae. Suddenly, with a quick, well-placed stomp, Daniil crushed the insect.

"Nooo!" I cried.

I pushed him brusquely, and he wobbled, taking a few steps back. With a crunch, the shell of the beetle had shattered, releasing a sticky brown liquid. Its head was still stuck to the sole of Daniil's shoe, which he was trying to clean off by stamping his foot like a horse.

"Are you crazy?" I said.

"Come on, Emma," said Gregory. "It's just a beetle. He didn't know."

"He did it on purpose!"

I clenched my fists and dug my nails into my palms. It felt like something important had just happened, but everyone else had already turned their attention back to the crackling fire. Night was falling. I stopped talking. Gregory began trying to teach the boys campfire songs.

We camped for three days. I couldn't stop thinking about the crushed beetle.

"CAN YOU TAKE THE BOYS TO GET THEIR HAIR CUT TODAY?" said Gregory as he finished his espresso.

After years of waiting, *Dwell Magazine* was finally going to include our house in its special issue on Canadian design. Lüke, a friend from the office, had gotten us the contract. The outside of our house wasn't of interest to Americans, but they wanted to feature our interior design in their Small Spaces section. We couldn't have hoped for better publicity. Gregory was over the moon; this was the key to the international market he'd been trying to break into for so long. He wanted everything to be perfect. I cocked my head and facetiously asked, "Do I look okay, or would you like me to go in and get a little Botox for the occasion?"

"You want to get Botox?" he said. "You know, Virginie got it, and you can't even tell."

"Then what good was it?" I muttered. But he didn't hear. He wasn't listening anyway.

"Take them to Blood & Bandages on College Street," he said. "Ask for Miles. I'll call and tell him how I want him to cut their hair."

He paced the floor as he spoke. The world revolved around him. I hadn't seen him so happy in a long time. He gave me a long kiss on the lips before leaving for work.

When I turned around, the twins were watching from the bend in the staircase like sentinels. Their hair had grown out in the six months they had been here and looked much better than their military cuts from the orphanage. Their hair was fine, but thick, with a gentle wave. Daniil's hair was more blond than his brother's, while Vanya's was more light brown. I hoped that Gregory hadn't decided to give them another short cut. I looked at the time and decided to get going. We'd walk, rather than taking the stroller.

College Street had changed in recent years. A number of hip establishments had replaced the Portuguese bars and cheap clothing stores. LIT Espresso, Baby on the Hip, Ziggy's at Home, and Bar Isabel had come out of the neighbourhood's recent gentrification.

We took a right and headed toward Ossington Avenue. It was early and not many stores were open, but it was nice to do a little window shopping. It was already hot and the streets smelled like dog shit. The twins walked slowly, zigzagging along the sidewalk. I had dressed them in simple shorts and T-shirts. It took us a solid half hour to cover the few metres to the salon.

Blood & Bandages looked like a typical hipster barbershop—reclaimed barn wood, black walls, vintage mirrors, and hunting trophies—but it also had magnificent Paidar barber chairs from the fifties, whose red leather had been meticulously maintained. Three young, tattooed, bearded barbers greeted us. The two other customers were dressed in the very same style.

"Hey, buddies!" said Miles, introducing himself to the boys with an extended hand. I realized, laughing to myself, that Gregory had the exact same haircut as his barber, whose hair was shaved on the sides and long on top, combed back.

"So we're going to give you daddy's haircut, boys?"

Gregory really had arranged everything in advance. I was relieved the boys would only be getting the sides trimmed.

It was decided that Daniil would go first. The barber put a board over the armrests of the chair to raise him up and attached a white paper band around his neck before draping the cape over his little shoulders. As Miles snipped his baby curls, Daniil looked down at his feet, avoiding his reflection in the mirror. From where he sat, Vanya watched as his brother's head underwent its change. He clenched his fists and I could see him panting with rage. I thought he was getting angry, but when his turn came, he let Miles dress him without protest. With his arms crossed under the cape, he watched the barber from the corner of his eye, his head pulled back into his neck. As he saw his haircut start to resemble his brother's, he relaxed.

Miles laughed at his seriousness and made small talk with me. I listened distractedly as he relayed that Gregory had told him all about the boys and he was happy to finally meet them.

"It's weird, they don't really look like twins, do they?" he said.

I nodded, so as not to contradict him. Everyone had their own opinion on whether they really looked like twins. To me, they had each looked distinctive for a while now, but every mother of twins feels that way.

The barber was just sweeping the last of the hair from Vanya's neck when he declared, shaking out the cape, "The Russian twins! Your daddy has told me so much about you. It's a pleasure to finally meet you, gentlemen."

He shook their hands as though they were adults. I gulped slowly. He had practically shouted it to the whole salon, and the other customers looked at me with revolting goodwill. I felt the blood drain from my cheeks and my hands turn to ice. I mumbled some thanks as I paid, before pushing the boys toward the exit. I might as well have soiled myself in front of everyone.

The following days were devoted to an intense cleaning of the whole house. *Dwell Magazine* didn't give its contributors much advance notice. We had only four days to get everything ready. I kept the house very clean, but I knew flashbulbs and professional lighting would forgive nothing, so I redoubled my efforts. As the week went on, I restricted the boys' access to certain rooms so they wouldn't mess them up.

"It's a good thing they're coming today," teased Gregory the morning of the shoot, "or you'd have relegated us all to the kitchen by now."

I was in no mood to laugh. The creative team was expected to arrive at ten o'clock, but I had gotten everyone out of bed at six and made a huge breakfast for the boys so they wouldn't get hungry in the middle of the shoot. Seeing my state, Gregory insisted I skip a second cup of coffee.

We argued over the outfits we would wear, as Gregory planned to have us all in matching striped T-shirts.

"Isn't that a little cliché?" I asked.

"Just make sure the kids don't have a meltdown," he said. "That's all I ask of you."

He wasn't kidding. I put on my striped shirt just for the sake of peace, and tried to avoid him until the *Dwell* crew arrived.

Molly, the artistic director, looked like she was about fourteen years old. She bent down excitedly and placed her hands on her thighs, bowing in front of the twins as though they were puppies.

"Oh my God, they are so cute! Look at them!" she squealed.

She introduced the crew by their first names: Cathy, Sam, Harlan, and Peisley. I wondered whether those were their real names or if they had changed them to be cool. They all made an effort to speak French to us, with the exception of Molly, who apparently hadn't mastered it. They were already bringing equipment into the front hall. They moved systematically; everything was organized, and they followed a strict order. The big trailer with the *Dwell* logo sat outside in front of the house. The neighbours slowed as they passed it, craning their necks when our front door opened. Gregory led the team upstairs. The twins had taken up position in front of the stairs with Jules, assessing the situation. Gregory's enthusiasm had started to take hold of me. I made espressos for everyone and got out the lemon cake I'd made.

"Is it gluten-free?" asked Molly, touching the cake. I'd given up on this kind of dietary restriction, since it didn't seem to have any influence on the children's behaviour.

"Uh, no," I said.

"Then I can't eat it," she said, turning on her heels without further comment. I stood looking at the slice of cake that still held the imprint of her finger. The rest of the team had finished their coffees and gotten back to work, leaving their dirty cups on the counter. I quickly cleaned everything up before joining them in the living room. I didn't know where to stand. Wherever I put myself, I was in the way.

The house's natural light was clearly insufficient for the photos and several big spotlights and reflectors had to be installed to augment the light. I congratulated myself on my impeccable cleaning. There were electrical wires crawling all over the floor and I had to be extra careful to make sure the twins didn't snag them with their feet. For each take, Peisley and Sam rethought the decor, repositioning items and furniture for optimal placement in the shot. With a painting in her hand, Peisley passed by me and gave me a little smile before laying it down flat on a shelf off-camera. Her job presumably was to pick out everything that met the standards of the magazine and get rid of everything that didn't. She was now scanning the buffet in the dining room, rolling up the sleeves of her plaid shirt. It was getting warm outside. I opened the window to the garden to let in a little fresh air. Peisley had chosen a Mexican skull painted in a *Día de Muertos* motif and moved it into the living room.

"Oh, that's perfect. Greg, hold it like you're talking to it."

He winked at me. I hated that they addressed him as Greg. Molly walked around him to get the right pose.

"Wait!"

Harlan moved away from his camera and Cathy stopped moving the reflective screens. Molly approached Gregory and, standing on her toes, ran a hand through his hair to push a strand back.

"Much better," she said excitedly.

Harlan resumed shooting Gregory, who was having fun, exaggerating his pose, looking toward the ceiling with a hand on his chin. The team thought he was funny. I stood with my back against the staircase, waiting my turn. On the stairs behind me, the twins sat sulkily, their faces pressed between the railings. Jules had taken up position between the two of them. As Molly reevaluated Gregory's pose, Harlan looked at the proofs on his screen. He was taking quick, sidelong glances at me. Suddenly, he turned to me and took a photo. I smiled timidly.

"Could you scooch over?" he whispered, waving the air with his hand.

I moved to the side, not understanding. He moved slowly, as though afraid of startling his prey. It was the twins and the cat he wanted, having spied them through the stairway railing. He smiled with satisfaction and turned back to Gregory. I lowered my eyes, blushing.

After a number of shots in the living room, Molly finally gave me a role in the kitchen: I was to serve the boys some orange juice in crystal glasses that enhanced the colour of the liquid.

"Tell them not to drink it," she said. "The juice can't get on the sides."

Gregory repeated the instructions, adding his critical assessment to the art direction. Seated side by side at the counter on stools, the boys fingered their glasses with no understanding of what was expected of them. They were being congratulated for not moving. They had to look at their juice, but weren't allowed to touch it. Gregory shouted encouragement as though they were accomplishing a great athletic feat.

"Can they, like, smile or something? They should look kind of happy. It is, like, the theme of this issue." Molly moved her head and shoulders as she spoke. Despite the heat, she wore a toque, spilling with long red curls. Behind Harlan, Gregory had started gesticulating to make the twins laugh. Thinking the he was supposed to imitate him, Daniil suddenly spread his arms, sweeping his glass to the ground with a smash.

"Oh my God, there's juice everywhere! Oh my God!" Molly shrieked, as the crew tried to mop up the liquid seeping through the electrical cords.

There were shards of wet glass all over the ground. It was hard to know where to even start cleaning.

"Emma, do something, don't just stand there like that. Go get the vacuum!" barked Gregory. "And put the cat somewhere, he's going to get hurt."

I sprang into action. Still sitting on their stools, the twins watched the scene, genuinely amused this time. Cathy panicked, thinking the juice had ruined one of her projectors. Harlan was sweating and didn't know where to set down his camera where it would be safe. Sam and Peisley were unrolling paper towels, laying them hurriedly on the ground. Molly was circling the mess. The house vibrated with such tension that when Sam sliced his hand on the broken glass, Vanya burst out laughing.

It was the last straw. Gregory smacked him across the face.

I froze, the vacuum hose in my hands. The whole team watched me. No one spoke. Gregory looked at me defiantly. My mind scrambled, I set down the vacuum and walked cautiously toward the twins. Vanya, his cheek scarlet, wasn't crying. I took them both gently by the hand to get them down from their stools, crossed the room silently with them, and left the house.

I set off walking aimlessly. It was a warm day for June. Once outside, I could breathe better. I refused to release the boys' hands no matter how they twisted in protest. I had to pull them to move them forward. When we had reached Dewson Street, I took out my phone to check the time: it was two-thirty in the afternoon. The boys would soon be hungry. I circled back around to Octopus Garden, a vegetarian café that made big tempeh sandwiches; that would keep the boys satisfied for a while. I decided we would take a picnic to Dufferin Grove Park. We went there all the time. It was a big wooded park, and the boys loved it. There seemed to be fewer rules here than in other parks in the city. The ambience was more geared to organic foods, farmers' markets, and outdoor theatre. The boho-chic parents there seemed less stressed than elsewhere. I checked the condition of Vanya's cheek: there was no mark.

As soon as we arrived, the boys jumped on the toys. In a gigantic natural sandbox, there was an array of shovels and wooden beams. Dozens of children were busy building canals and bridges in the filthy sand. A kind of urban savagery reigned, which pleased everyone. They could play here for hours without ever worrying about me. Sitting on a big tree trunk that was used as a bench, I watched them muddy the expensive Salt-Water sandals and striped shirts Gregory had chosen for them.

"Are they twins?"

It was always the same introduction. I shook myself from my stupor and asserted proudly that they were. The man next to me was tanned and sporty. He was bottle-feeding a baby while holding the leash of a woolly puppy. His eyes were fixed on a spot in the distance; he was also watching an older child. His name was Oliver, and he spoke calmly in a deep voice with a Welsh accent. We made a little small talk and I quickly learned that he had an engineering degree, but was a stay-at-home dad. His wife was a doctor at the Women's College Hospital. I gawked before managing to overcome my surprise.

"When do you see yourself returning to work?" I asked, curious, but trying to seem nonchalant. I had never met a stay-at-home father.

"I don't think I'll go back to work. Michelle often works seventy-hour weeks," said Oliver, skilfully wiping the milk dribbling down the baby's chin. "Mathilde will be starting kindergarten in September," he continued, pointing out a little girl in sporty shorts and a baseball cap. "My days will be a little less busy then."

The little girl joined the group of drillers. The twins unquestioningly accepted her into the group. Because of her outfit, they must have mistaken her for a boy; normally they wanted nothing to do with girls.

Oliver told me candidly about his life, and asked me questions in turn. An hour later, without even meaning to, I'd told him about the twins' adoption, their troubled personalities, and the failure of the *Dwell* photoshoot. Realizing the magnitude of what I'd shared, I abruptly declared that we had to go. I packed up my bag and my muddy boys in one swift manoeuvre.

When I got home, the house was silent. The *Dwell* crew were gone, leaving no trace of their presence. Gregory was sitting at the table, finishing dinner. The boys had eaten late, and weren't interested in the meal I offered to make them. So I took them straight upstairs to give them a bath, ignoring Gregory. Then I took my time reading them a story and tucking them in, before going back down to the kitchen. I was waiting to hear how Gregory would explain himself.

"They were very professional finishing up the session. The photos are going to work out. They'll even be able to save the ones of the boys before the incident," he said, ending lightly on the word.

He was happy. I was stunned.

"Good call leaving with the kids," he said. "It turned out to be much easier without them around." He kissed me on the cheek and went downstairs to watch TV.

I noisily put his abandoned dishes in the dishwasher and blew the crumbs off the table. When I was finished, I cast a last glance around me: everything was impeccable. I got out the pack of Armenian papers, carefully detached a strip, and folded it in a perfect zigzag before lighting one end with the lighter. I placed the paper in its terra cotta cup, and leaned my hip against the counter as I watched the plumes of incense dissipate into the air. The spicy fragrance tickled my nostrils. Then I went upstairs. I had no desire to join Gregory in the basement.

It was late. The boys had fallen fast asleep, spent after the day's drama. As I did every night, I went into their room to make sure they were sleeping soundly before going to bed myself. Two Heico nightlights cast an orange glow over the room. Each of the boys was sleeping with his stuffed toy at the end of the bed: the striped cat for Daniil and the monkey for Vanya. Their identical wrought-iron beds and night tables sat symmetrically on either side of the big window, separated by a shag rug where Jules lay watchfully.

Even asleep, the boys' features held the shadow of concern; they never seemed entirely at peace. Daniil furrowed his brow in his sleep, and jerked his shoulders. Vanya slept on his stomach, his head turned toward his brother, breathing with his mouth open. I pulled up the covers around Daniil, and knelt for a moment at Vanya's side, tilting my head at the same angle as his. A gentle snore escaped his lips. I brought my face close to his and closed my eyes to inhale his baby's breath. I stayed this way for a few minutes, taking advantage of the intimacy of nighttime, then tiptoed out.

In the bathroom mirror, I began the process of washing my face. I warmed cream in my palms before rubbing it on my face and neck. My skin turned shiny and supple. I started with light touches on my forehead, eyes, and chin. I continued with the pressure points for lymphatic drainage. With my eyes closed, I moved my fingers in gentle but firm circles to smooth out frown lines, crow's feet, and smile lines. I lingered on my lips, rolling the flesh between my fingers, playing with their elasticity. I controlled the movement to maintain precision, without crossing into pain. I finished off with some light pinching on my eyebrows and jawline with the pads of my fingers. I repeated the motions several times until I felt a shiver down my spine. The oil penetrated my skin, lubricated it, and melted gently. I cleaned off the excess with a cotton pad, relaxed and purified.

IN THE NEXT WEEKS, we often went back to Dufferin Grove. Summer was in full swing and the food stand was open. We could buy cookies and coffee, and at lunchtime they served hot dogs and mac and cheese. It wasn't an ideal diet, but it saved me from cooking and the boys loved comfort food.

They weren't fighting with other children anymore. I had patiently explained to them that they would never make friends if they kept throwing sand at them and knocking them down. From then on, they isolated themselves and only played with each other, but at least they had stopped harassing others.

Gregory's parents finally decided to come visit and were arriving the next day, since it was Canada Day and Gregory was off work. They were going to spend four days in Toronto. Gregory invited them to stay at the house, but they said they would rather stay in a hotel and booked a room at a cheap Holiday Inn on Carlton Street. I had talked to them a few times on the phone and they seemed eager to meet the boys. I'd tried to introduce them on Skype, but the call ended up being very artificial. The boys didn't recognize the faces talking to them and couldn't respond, because they were barely speaking. The few calls I'd managed to have with my parents were just as unsuccessful, but at least I avoided having them come to the house.

While I supervised the twins splashing in the wading pool, I made a list on my phone of the things I still had to buy before the arrival of my in-laws:

Flowers
Baguette
White wine
Oysters
Skim milk

"Hello."

Oliver, the stay-at-home father, was standing before me. He was directly blocking the sun and I had to squint to look at him, blinded. I smiled, peering through slitted eyes. I must have looked ridiculous.

"The kids aren't with you?" I asked.

"Oh sure, they're right over there," he said, pointing to the little girl in bathing shorts, holding her brother's hand as he moved uncertainly, his feet in the water.

I didn't know what to say to him. I was still uncomfortable from the last time, and I stupidly hoped he had forgotten the secrets I'd told him.

"How is your wife?" I asked, saying the first thing that came to mind.

"She's well, but she's working in intensive care this week. It's hard," he said calmly, not seeming to notice my nervousness.

"I was about to get a coffee," he said. "Would you like one?"

"Absolutely!" I replied with schoolgirl enthusiasm. I don't know why he had this effect on me. Granted, he was a good-looking man, but still. He was already on his way back with two recycled cardboard cups.

"I tried to guess how you take it. I gave you a little milk and a little sugar. Is that okay?"

He really was charming.

"That's perfect, thank you. Oh! Coffee! I also have to get coffee. Forgive me, my husband's parents are arriving tomorrow and I still have a ton of things to pick up. They haven't met the boys yet."

Here I was again, showcasing my life for him.

"This is an important visit, then. Do they have other grandchildren?" he asked.

"Yes, my husband's brother has four girls."

"Four! He's a brave man. I've got my hands full with two."

It was strange talking to a man with the same daily routine as me. The boys got out of the pool, their lips blue.

"Oh my—that water is cold!" I cried.

They weren't shivering, but I rubbed vigorously as I towelled them off. I was about to take off their wet bathing suits, but they gave me a scowl that stopped me cold. They had never showed any modesty before; it must have been Oliver's presence that embarrassed them.

"Excuse me, Oliver, we have to go. Thanks for the coffee."

I put the twins in the stroller, letting them warm up in their towels and piling their clothes into the basket under Daniil's seat. Since leaving the orphanage, we had kept the same arrangement: I always put Vanya in the top seat, Daniil below. There looked to be enough room in the string basket for the things I had to buy. If I was lucky, the twins would sleep through my errands.

I pushed the stroller all over town for several hours, getting everything I needed, sweating as it grew heavier and heavier. When I finally got home, the boys were howling with impatience. We were all dirty and tired and I couldn't wait to take a shower. Then I noticed the car.

They were already here.

I didn't even make it up the driveway before Gregory and my in-laws were already out on the porch.

"We decided to come a day early!"

I could feel the sweat on my cheeks as my mother-in-law kissed them.

"They've got quite a set of lungs!" said my father-in-law jovially.

I tried to undo the straps of the stroller to release the children. I hadn't had a chance to dress them after the park, but at least they were diapered. Under the watchful eye of my in-laws, I forgot the correct order in which to do things: I tried to get the boys out of the stroller at the same time as all the groceries. Finally, Gregory came to help me bring everything in, throwing the wet clothes in the front hall and carrying the groceries to the kitchen.

"Excuse us, we're just going to go clean up. I'll just be a minute," I said.

I was about to escape upstairs when my mother-in-law started following me up.

"I'll help you."

I stared back and tried to smile. "That's sweet, but you don't have to. I'll be right down."

"Not at all. You take your shower, I'll take care of them."

I didn't know how to get rid of her. We were squeezed into the middle of the staircase. She tried to take the boys by the hand, but they escaped to their bedroom, growling.

"They're shy," I said.

"I see that," she said with disappointment, finally giving up on following us.

I wiped the boys' faces, dressed them in clean clothes, and quickly showered before making my way to the living room. I took the stairs slowly, holding the boys' hands.

"Monique, André, this is Daniil and Vanya."

My mother-in-law, wiggling a finger, invited them to sit next to her on the couch. I tried to bring them closer, but they wouldn't budge from the foot of the stairs.

"They're still uncomfortable around new people." I tried to pull them by the hand, but they resisted.

"We're going to let you get used to everyone, okay?" I didn't insist, because I knew it was pointless to force them.

"Well then," I said. "What can I get you to drink? We have beer, white wine, I can make you a kir…"

"I'll take a 7UP, if you have one," Monique interrupted.

Yes, I did. I knew my mother-in-law and had filled the cupboards with soft drinks, even though I'd hoped that time would have loosened her up.

"I'll take a coffee," said André.

"Espresso or cappuccino?" I pressed my lips together.

"A what? A normal coffee will do," stammered my father-in-law.

"We don't have regular coffee," I said. "We only have an espresso maker."

He was already starting to get to me. Gregory laid a hand on my shoulder and said, "It's okay, Dad. I'll make you an Americano. It's just like your drip coffee, you'll see."

When I met them over ten years ago, André was built like a football player, straight-backed and swaggering, while Monique had a pin-up figure, well-endowed and slim-waisted. It was hard to recognize that couple in the one here today. Monique had been a career cashier at a Provigo and André had been an accountant at a small firm. Both retired, they still lived in the bungalow in Sainte-Foy, Quebec, where they'd raised Gregory and his brother, Ian.

The boys had approached the living room and were rolling on the ground with a meowing Jules.

"What language do they speak?" asked André, raising his voice since I was still in the kitchen.

"They don't really talk," I said. "They listen, for now."

"How can they not be talking? They're almost two, aren't they? Ian's girls were speaking in full sentences at one year," added my mother-in-law.

"Yes, but Ian's girls aren't bilingual, Mom."

"That's true... And your brother was late talking, unlike you. I notice nothing has changed in your case..."

I was neither surprised, nor disappointed, nor angry. I cast a cynical look at the clock: it had taken them less than an hour to say something disparaging about the adoption. I looked at the maraschino cherry rolling around the bottom of the glass of 7UP. A mass of little bubbles created a second skin on the fruit. I poured myself a glass of white wine and returned to the living room with the drinks. We said nothing to them about the twins' withdrawal, it goes without saying.

We looked at each other and raised our glasses, smiles frozen on our lips. "Cheers!"

My mother-in-law tried in vain to get the children to come to her. "Come and see Grandma. Look, I brought you a surprise!" she said.

She reached in her bag and pulled out two coloured yo-yos. The boys rose together as one, looked at her for a moment, and walked over to take the toys.

"We say 'thank you,' boys," I said limply.

Obviously, they didn't repeat it. Ineptly working the yo-yo, Vanya unrolled the whole string in one throw, causing the metal base to bounce off the floor. Jules leapt on it instantly, clawing at it with glee. The next moment, Daniil unrolled his to give the cat a second quarry. Jules jumped joyfully from one to the other under the crestfallen eye of my mother-in-law. The twins then ran up the stairs, dragging the yo-yos behind them so that Jules would chase them. They had disappeared into their room, but we could still hear the yo-yos knocking against the furniture upstairs. Monique probably expected me to intervene, but I had no intention of saving her crap. If it amused the cat, it would keep them occupied for a moment.

"So it isn't too much? Two at the same time can't be easy."

My mother-in-law was trying to make conversation with me while Gregory and his father discussed hockey.

"No, no, everything's going fine," I said nonchalantly.

"They seem a little... wild, don't they?"

She talked about them as though they were animals. I took a big gulp of wine to calm myself, and said, "They're just babies. It's a lot of change for them to adapt to."

"Sure, sure, but still. They've been with you for six months. I was expecting them to be a little more... well... I don't know... At any rate, they seem very independent. A year and a half is young to be playing alone in their room, isn't it?"

"These days, it's considered important that children develop independence. It's essential for developing leadership skills."

I didn't want to credit her words, but I nonetheless wondered what the boys were doing in their room. We hadn't heard any noise at all for a while. I kept sipping my Riesling.

"Emma, where are the boys anyway? We came here to see them and they're nowhere to be found!" cried André.

I raised my eyebrows and blinked. André had always been a simple, rude man, and now he had the physique to match his personality.

"But of course," I said, "You're missing the main attraction! I'll go get them."

He missed my sarcasm, giving me a big, cheerful smile in response. I couldn't help but roll my eyes. I set my wine glass down on the coffee table and went upstairs.

When I opened the door, it took me a moment to understand what I was seeing. The floor was covered in a fluffy substance, like a synthetic snow, in which Jules was playing. What had this stuffing come from? The boys were sitting on their beds, their hair full of tufts. Their stuffed animals—they had decapitated them. The torn casings of the cat and the striped monkey lay on the ground, empty.

I screamed in horror, which brought the others running.

"My God, what is that?"

André and Monique stood in the doorway as though the room was a war zone. I pulled myself together quickly.

"Oh, it's nothing, just an accident. I'll go get the vacuum. Don't worry, boys, we'll get you more stuffies."

What's more, they didn't seem in the least bit sorry. I cleaned up in a hurry.

"All right, I think everyone is hungry," I said. "I'll start dinner. I'm sorry, it won't be fancy—we weren't expecting you until tomorrow. We have oysters, and I can make a pasta with fresh tomatoes."

"The babies eat oysters?" asked Monique, intrigued.

"No, they can't eat that kind of thing raw. I have smoked salmon for them."

"Isn't smoked salmon also raw?"

"No, Monique. Smoked salmon is smoked."

"Of course, but you see what I mean."

I didn't see.

"More 7UP, Monique?" The wine was quashing my inhibitions and I was feeling frisky.

The twins behaved themselves at dinner, even if they didn't respond to the silly questions their grandparents asked them. Gregory was shockingly low-key. Just as we were finishing up the meal, my mother-in-law announced that they were going to turn in.

"Yes, it's the babies' bedtime too," I said, bursting out laughing.

I'd had a little too much to drink. Gregory stood loudly up from the table to see his parents off. I composed myself and helped the boys down from their chairs.

"Come on, let's say goodbye to Grandma and Grandpa."

I tried to pull myself together. I could sense that Gregory was angry. We promised to see each other early the next morning. As soon as the door had closed behind them, Gregory turned violently to me.

"You think I don't know what you're doing, Emma?"

"Listen, I have nothing against your parents, but I think it's a little early for the boys—they're not ready to meet the family."

"It's your fault if they don't know how to socialize. Look at what you've become. You need to get help, Emma, because this will not do."

I waved a hand to let him know I didn't feel like fighting. The wine had gone to my head, and I decided to go to bed as well.

As soon as his parents left Toronto, I knew Gregory would pick up the debate right where he'd left off. Nonetheless, the remainder of their visit went well. My in-laws made the return trip between their hotel and our house each day, and we were able to stroll around the neighbourhood with them. The boys were generally good with their grandparents, but I got the feeling Monique and André left disappointed.

I resented their small-mindedness. Our children were different, but every day I saw more indications of exceptional personalities. It was with this mindset that I agreed to meet with a support group, thinking that if my children were to reach their full potential, I might need a hand, just as Gregory thought.

During the adoption process, we'd been given a number of pamphlets, among which was one for the APAR, the Association of Parents Adopting in Russia. The irony of the acronym made me laugh. The building in which APAR held their meetings was in the very heart of Trinity Bellwoods Park. It was very close to the house, so I could walk there. I planned to play in the park with the children after the meeting.

A long ramp provided access downstairs to the main room for wheelchairs and strollers. The incline was steep and the weight of the Phil & Teds stroller dragged me perilously forward.

"Let me help you!" offered a blond woman approaching at a run.

As she held the stroller, the woman introduced herself, welcomed me, and complimented me on my beautiful boys. I released the twins and parked the Phil & Teds in a corner with the others. Feeling out of place, I kept my distance for a moment.

Some effort had gone into livening up the room with craft tables and coloured rugs, but the space was no less dour. Vanya and Daniil right away spotted a wading pool filled with plastic balls and made their way clamorously to it.

A number of mothers stood next to the coffee table, chatting. I moved discreetly into the group, clutching my polystyrene cup. Snippets of conversation drifted out, juxtaposing maternal stories. I glanced over and saw that the boys had moved on to the drawing table.

The family models were interchangeable. Shauna had adopted a deaf boy from Moscow, who was now in therapy.

Yannick had a boy, also from Moscow, with serious attachment issues. Marie's boy was autistic and often violent with her biological daughter. I was surprised how happy I was to hear stories worse than my own.

When my turn came, the mothers were so excited at my luck of adopting twins that the story of their withdrawal went unnoticed. In the eyes of these women, my problems were minor.

I was interrupted by a cry. We turned to see that a little girl had stolen Daniil's drawings. What happened next took only a second, and I watched helplessly as the whole scene unfolded in what felt like a slow-motion scene from a bad movie. Daniil brandished a pencil, held it up in the air, and brought it right down into the little girl's hand. The blunt tip only penetrated her flesh by a few millimetres, but Daniil held his grip fast. We all shrieked and rushed to our children. I had to wrench the pencil from Daniil's hands.

I briskly pulled the boys away, gripping them both firmly by the shoulder so they didn't escape. I forced them to stay seated beside me.

"Do you want me to call an ambulance?" My voice was weak and raspy.

One of the mothers took off her silk scarf and wrapped it around the girl's hand.

"I wonder if the nerve is severed."

"Can she still move her fingers?"

The women shot judgmental looks at me as they spoke. I had a sour taste in my mouth and my tongue stuck to my palate. I let out a loud burp, but no one heard. Hot saliva pooled in my mouth. I was going to throw up. I closed my eyes, trying to contain my nausea.

The mother of the little girl didn't want to call emergency services, but she called her husband and asked him to come.

I wanted to run away. I had to stay, however, until the issue was resolved. I had not let go of the boys' hands; I had to show that I had them under control. Furthermore, they made no effort to break away. Vanya played with the Velcro on his shoes and Daniil sucked his thumb. I released their hands for a moment to fix their hair. They looked like savage children with their unruly mops. We had just been to the barber a few weeks earlier, but their hair was growing out at an unreasonable rate.

The father arrived in a panic, letting the door slam behind him. He wore a blue suit with a loud tie. He had clearly come from work. He went straight to his little girl to examine the wound. I couldn't see how she was doing from the distance where we sat, but she started crying twice as hard at her father's approach.

"Who did this?" he roared, scanning the room.

All eyes turned toward us, secluded in our corner. I wrapped an arm protectively around the boys and brought them closer.

"It was an accident. He's not even two years old." I said this without indicating which of the twins had done it, holding them both against my chest. "I'll give you my contact information," I continued miserably.

"We'll be fine," the father cut in, lifting up his little girl, still loudly crying.

"Hold on, just in case there are any after-effects, give us your card," ordered the mother, suddenly hostile.

I had to confess that I had no longer had a business card.

"That doesn't surprise me," she spat. "We'll find you through the Association, if we need to."

An embarrassed silence followed the aggrieved family's departure. The other mothers all swiftly took their leave, avoiding my gaze.

When everyone had gone, I backed my way up the access ramp. This time, no one came to my aid.

"He's a baby," Gregory went on. "Those mothers should have been more understanding."

"It was so awful," I said.

We had already spent the whole week talking about the incident, but nothing had been resolved.

"It wasn't malice, it was impulsiveness. You're impulsive sometimes too."

I said nothing: it was my fault again. I turned my attention to the road whipping by, and forced myself not to cry in front of the children. Gregory was dropping us off at the little farm in Riverdale that morning. It was on his way to work, since the office was further east on Danforth Avenue.

"In any case, I'm not setting foot in another of those meetings. I never want to see those women again."

At least on that point, Gregory agreed. The little I'd seen of the meeting before the catastrophe hadn't convinced me of its usefulness. "Maybe we should send them to a psychiatrist."

We'd arrived at Riverdale Farm. Gregory parked diagonally and watching the boys in the rearview mirror as they wriggled in their seats. They were covered in Cheerios.

"No, Emma, I'm not putting them in the hands of a specialist who's going to find some kind of problem and give them drugs. All the kids these days come out of those consultations with some kind of diagnosis: ADD, ADHD, OCD, Tourette's, oppositional defiant disorder, language disorder... It's absurd, and I don't want any of it. We're their parents, it's up to us to help them to grow, to integrate, to learn. And it's mainly you doing that work, I know that very well. I know it's hard. That's why I wanted you to go get help, but you're a very good mother. I have faith in you. We don't need a psychologist."

I suddenly felt important. Yes, I was able to educate our sons. I could do it. I hugged Gregory and got out of the car, ready to have an excellent day.

We waved to Gregory in the car as he drove away, and I helped the boys put on their little backpacks.

"So, boys, what would you like to see first? The pigs? The cows? The sheep?"

Daniil looked elsewhere and Vanya chewed his top lip. I knew they knew the words, because I had just spent the whole week reading farm-related books with them and I had directed all our games with farm figurines. It simply wasn't possible that they didn't understand.

"Vanya, what would you like?"

I waited a long time for him to answer.

"Cow."

He said it clearly, looking me right in the eye. No, there was no way he knew it was an insult. I immediately dismissed the notion.

"Bravo, Vanya! Let's go see the cows then."

Every word they spoke was a triumph worthy of acclaim. I took them by the hand and headed off, skipping. There were lovely flowers decorating the farm, and the buildings were separated by hilly roads. A number of groups with excited children moved from one enclosure to another. The farm was managed by the City of Toronto. The staff worked languidly, there to both answer visitors' questions and take care of the animals. The smell of soil and animals permeated our clothes.

The cows were not in the stable, but were grazing in a nearby enclosure. The boys squatted down to pass their arms through the fence.

"Careful, she can bite."

Daniil stood back up, but Vanya stayed in the very same position and grabbed some hay from the ground. Lowering her big muzzle, the cow sniffed Vanya's hand before licking up the whole handful of straw. The two boys burst out laughing. Vanya wiped his hand on his shorts and Daniil came to join him and grab a new tuft of straw. The cow licked them each in turn, seemingly glad to be fed.

The twins were so overwhelmed with uproarious laughter that they fell over backwards. I had never seen them so happy. I laughed with them at the animal's voracity.

"Well, she seems to like you very much."

They paid no attention to me at all, not appearing to have heard what I had said. Daniil had put his arm around his brother and they laughed with one voice. I stood back to get a picture of them in that pose, and texted it to Gregory to show him what fun we were having. Then I sat on a bench a little distance from them, since it was impossible to make them leave the pen; they didn't want to visit anything else. I took out my tube of hand cream and started massaging my cuticles as I watched them. They had gotten down on their hands and knees and were pretending to chew, shaking their heads to chase away the flies themselves. Other children regularly came over to stand at the fence, but they didn't stay interested for long. They watched the ruminants for a few moments, then left. I shared a smile with the mother or the Filipino nanny accompanying them.

They spent the entire morning with one particular cow, following her as she moved across her cramped enclosure. There were three cows, but theirs, a big red one, never moved from the fence where they perched. The special bond they had with Jules seemed to extend to other animals; they were more gifted in establishing relationships with animals than with other children, I thought wryly. I suggested to them numerous times that we continue with our visit, but, seeing how happy they were, I didn't insist. We didn't see a single other animal that day.

"Would you boys like me to take a photo of you with your cow?" I asked when it was time to leave.

Since they didn't seem to understand why, I added, "We can have it printed and hang it in your room."

They'd stopped laughing. I half-heartedly took a photo anyway, trying to frame them with the animal. The photo hung for several months on the wall of their room. They never paid it the slightest attention.

THEIR BIRTHDAY WAS COMING UP, the first one they would be celebrating with us. I wanted an intimate party, but Gregory had other ideas.

"There are so many people who still haven't met them—everyone from the office, the neighbours... We could have a big party and invite everyone. Then you wouldn't have to go around introducing them individually."

I didn't like the idea at all. I thought back to the chaos of the *Dwell Magazine* shoot and was not eager to repeat it. On the other hand, those people had all given us gifts after the adoption. I would eventually have to do the polite thing and introduce our children. Perhaps Gregory was right; I would save myself some trouble by inviting everyone at once. I took a few days to think about it, wavering between the idea of the big gathering and the small one with just us.

I finally came around to Gregory's point of view. Up to a point, it had been acceptable to isolate the boys—to give them time to adapt—but after too long, people would start to ask questions. So I set to designing invitations, and quickly found myself with a list of over thirty people. We were close with four of our colleagues at the firm. With their families, we were already at sixteen people. Two neighbourhood couples, one of whom had two children, had given me gifts; another six guests. With Magalie, her husband, and their son, I had twenty-five. With the four of us, that made twenty-nine, thirteen of whom were children under ten. I had a moment of dread thinking about the planning, until I started to think of it as a corporate event. All I had to do was feed and entertain a few adults and children for a few hours, which wasn't that hard.

I could see no way of cooking effectively for that number of people, so I strapped the boys into their stroller and set off for Nadège on Queen Street. The bakery's catering service was expensive, but very elegant.

As soon as I arrived, they led me to a banquette near the patio and offered me a Kusmi tea. A young staff member in the store's pink apron presented me with an iPad listing all the different options. Another staff member took the boys by the hand and brought them to see the kitchen, where the macaroons were prepared behind a big bay window. I chose a hundred hors d'oeuvres topped with smoked salmon, foie gras, camembert, and sausage, and even indulged in one of their *pièces montées* as a birthday cake. I charged the bill to the firm and left, quite pleased with my organizing skills, carrying a pink box filled with sample treats.

I took advantage of being on Queen Street to go into the Paper Place, which was just across the street. The shop carried a wide variety of delicate papers and prints, as well as stationery. I perused the narrow aisles until the boys got impatient and threatened to grab the expensive wrapping paper within their reach. I hurried to the cash with garlands and paper lanterns. I had no intention of decorating the house with hideous helium balloons that would only end up popping in the midst of the excitement.

I still had to come up with an activity to liven up the party. Outdoor games were out of the question, as it was October and much too cold. Indoor games would have to do. I remembered the birthday games my parents planned for us: Pin the Tail on the Donkey, mini-bowling, hula-hoop contests... but the twins were too young for that kind of activity, and those games were out of fashion anyway.

On our way home, we stopped by Trinity Bellwoods Park and I watched the boys play amongst the other children, indifferent to them. I thought then of an activity involving animals. I knew of companies that brought in different creatures—chinchillas and guinea pigs and the like—for children's birthday parties. It seemed perfect to me, and would be good for children of all ages. By the time Gregory got home from work, the party was planned. I was bursting with pride at my efficiency.

The morning of the birthday, everything was ready: the decorations were up, I had picked up my order at Nadège, and the entertainment had been prepaid.

Guests were scheduled to arrive at three, after the twins' nap. The morning went well. I finished cleaning the house and had time to get ready and get the boys dressed. Gregory tried to get them excited, telling them about the party, all the guests coming to see them, and all the gifts they would get. The boys didn't understand, but the more Gregory hyped up the party, the more tormented I felt about people meeting my sons.

I frantically scoured the house to make sure everything was impeccable. I knew that all eyes would be on my actions as a mother, judging my competence and capacity to manage both the children and the guests. We had often thrown parties at the house for our colleagues or friends in the past and I had a reputation as an excellent hostess. Glasses were always full, food was exquisite, and the music and ambience were of the highest order. Would I live up to those expectations?

My confidence was crumbling and the guests would start arriving dangerously soon. Perhaps having sensed my anxiety, the boys woke up from their nap nervous and irritable. They cried over nothing and I was so frustrated with Vanya that I ended up having to give him a time-out.

As soon as I had closed the door to his bedroom, I realized the preposterousness of the whole situation. I had spent the week neglecting and excluding the boys so that I could plan an elaborate party to delight my friends and showcase my mothering abilities. But no one would be fooled. It would be clear to everyone that my sons had no connection to me. Everyone would see it. My incompetence would be revealed to the world. I would make a spectacle of myself and become gossip fodder for months to come. I had sacrificed my career to take care of them, but I was a failure as a mother.

The truth was that those boys were nothing like other children: they didn't talk. They were violent, inadequate, isolated. I was already bracing for the worst. They would assault another child, or an animal, howl or hurt themselves, and I wouldn't know how to control them. This party was a horrible mistake.

I was pacing the upstairs hallway and didn't hear Gregory come up the stairs.

"Emma, what are you doing?" he said. "Come on, quit tearing your hair out like that. Have you had a look at your head? Go to the bedroom and calm down. The guests will be here any minute."

He pushed me toward our bed and ordered me to pull myself together. A violent migraine had come on and I curled up in a ball to ease the pain.

I heard Gregory welcoming the first guests. I tried to raise myself up on one elbow, but the pressure in my skull was so powerful that my head fell right back on my pillow. I couldn't move. My whole body was in pain. I could feel my joints grinding.

The doorbell rang incessantly. I heard laughs and cries, and I fought to stay awake. They needed me; I couldn't fall asleep. I had to get downstairs and get the party in order, but I was paralyzed in my bed. Holding my head with both hands, I pressed on my temples to try and ease the pain. I concentrated on my breath, took a few deep, slow inhalations. It took a moment, but the controlled breathing started working and my migraine receded little by little. I opened my eyes.

I could see nothing at all.

Blackness, everywhere. Panting, I blinked several times, rubbing my eyelids. I was blind. I looked around the room and could make out nothing, not a sliver of light. I covered my eyes with my palms and started screaming for Gregory.

Only a whisper emerged from my mouth. My throat was parched and burning. But I had to find the strength to call Gregory, I could have been having a heart attack.

"Gregory! GREGORY!"

His hand gripped my shoulder forcefully, his thumb in the divot of my clavicle. Gregory was shirtless, lying beside me. He had turned on the bedside lamp, throwing a dim light on our room.

"Where were you?" I said. "I thought I was having a heart attack."

"Emma, I'm here. It's two-thirty in the morning. Go to sleep."

"But... the party?"

"You missed it, Emma. I tried to wake you up, but you pushed me away and said you wanted to sleep. So sleep. I'm tired too, you know."

"The guests came? The children got their cake? And the activities with the animals?"

"Emma, the birthday is over. Yes, they got their presents, their cake, everything."

"And there were no problems?"

"No, everything went fine. I've had enough, Emma. Go to sleep, okay? We'll talk about it tomorrow."

Gregory turned out the light and I lay there staring into the dark room, my eyes adjusting to the blackness.

I received a number of emails the next day from friends, hoping I was feeling better, congratulating me on the lovely birthday party. Magalie even attached some photos of the children with the animals, the twins opening their gifts, blowing out their candles. Scrolling through the pictures, I burst out sobbing. It was their first birthday with us and I had missed everything.

Throughout the next year, I often thought of that birthday; I didn't want to miss another thing. Gregory and I talked about the possibility of home-schooling the boys. We had admitted that our children were different, and that their uniqueness was worth preserving.

I started reading a ton of articles and books on the benefits of home-schooling. By educating them this way, I could reinforce the lessons and adapt to their needs, and we would still have time for hobbies and exercise. Everything I read about home-schooled children suggested that they were more gifted than others, and sharper intellectually.

The majority of the mothers I started communicating with in the chat rooms split their days in two: they devoted the morning to lessons and the afternoon to cultural activities and sports. And so I started initiating the twins into this system; for the first half of the day, they did preschool exercises, and for the other half, we visited museums and went to recreation centres or to the pool. At this pace, in a few months, they began speaking distinctly in French and English, and managed to channel their energy through sports—particularly swimming—at which they showed a real aptitude. Gregory was very happy with their progress and credited me with every improvement in their behaviour. We agreed that we had been right to integrate them differently, given that there were two of them. It wasn't as though they were completely isolated.

They played together increasingly well, moreover, and in this respect seemed more advanced than children their age. From the time they were nearly three years old, they knew how to play a number of board games, and when they played dress-up, could stay in character for hours. They fought rarely, but when they did, they were violent. One day while they were playing with Duplo blocks, Daniil accidentally stepped on a part of their construction. Vanya, furious, hit his brother so hard that he lost his balance and fell backwards, knocking his head against the cabinet behind him. I leapt in to comfort him, even though he wasn't really crying. Instead, he fixed Vanya with a look of such intense hatred, hard to imagine in a child so young. But they always made up quickly and picked up their game where they had left off.

My schooling program became more and more rigorous over the months, as the twins were responding to it so well. They easily picked up new material and motor skills. They learned the alphabet, the days of the week, the months and seasons, their numbers up to—and even past—one hundred, the names of animals, trees, and fruit, and how to locate Toronto on the globe. The letters they traced were more and more precise and we were starting to combine them to spell words.

However, despite my best efforts, their initiation to reading had been difficult. They made no connection with the stories whatsoever. They didn't identify with the protagonists and couldn't understand their reactions. I tried to get them interested in hundreds of books, even turning to traditional Russian stories, thinking that they might relate to them more, without success. They paid no attention to the stories and retained nothing. They couldn't answer a single question on any text, and didn't seem to understand them, but I knew they were capable of more complex learning.

This strange resistance was confirmed one night when Gregory finally came home with the issue of *Dwell Magazine*. We were on the cover. Gregory was in a fever; he held off opening it all day, even as his colleagues lavished him with compliments. He'd waited for us to look at it together.

Ceremoniously, he made us sit on the living room sofa. He carefully opened the magazine. Our article, at seven pages long, was the main feature of the issue. Everything was perfect. Our design was captured at the best angles, our aesthetic was clearly defined and, against our magnificent decor, our family sparkled. Gregory had been right about the stripes for our clothes, which made us stand out even as we blended in with the clean lines of the design. The team of journalists who'd interviewed us had made an excellent selection of our statements. It would be a big publicity boost.

Hunched over the pages, the twins moved through the photos with their fingers as though to read the subtitles of the illustrations. But no story seemed to materialize for them in the pictures.

"Is that me?" asked Daniil, pointing to a picture of his brother.

I smiled. "No, my love. That's you," I said, sliding his finger to his own image.

Vanya shot a look at his brother from the corner of his eye, and both of them, in one voice, countered me with a cold, conclusive, "No."

They'd already lost interest in me, but I couldn't take my eyes off them. How did they see themselves? As one person? They turned the pages of the magazine roughly, as Gregory tried to make them focus on certain photos. A thought stopped me that turned my blood to ice. They didn't see themselves as one person; they saw themselves as the *other*. Daniil identified as Vanya, and Vanya as Daniil. I leapt from the chair and ran to get a mirror in the bathroom. I held it briskly out to Daniil.

"Who's that?"

The twins had let go of the magazine, but still didn't respond. Gregory didn't understand what I was doing.

"Daniil, who's that in the mirror?"

I held his shoulder so he could concentrate. He backed up and pressed against his brother.

"Daniil! Answer me!"

"Come on, Emma, what's wrong with you? You're scaring him."

"Let me do this, Gregory, it's important. Daniil, look here: who's the little boy in the mirror?"

He curled up in a ball with Vanya, their two bodies forming a compact shell. I couldn't get through.

"What are you trying to prove, Emma?"

"I... I thought they had mixed themselves up..." I said, catching my breath.

"But that's normal, Emma, they're twins. Babies don't even recognize themselves in the mirror."

"Yes, but they're nearly three years old... And it's not even as though they look that much alike..."

They were still locked together, staring stonily at me, white-lipped.

Gregory was so impressed by the boys' progress that he overlooked their eccentricities. From a scholarly point of view, it's true that they were advanced for their age, and Gregory took every opportunity to brag about it at the firm.

"Philip thinks they're gifted, like his daughter. That would explain their social difficulties. Those children often have a hard time integrating, because they're superior to the others."

The idea that my boys were exceptional filled me with fierce pride. From that point on, I looked at them differently, feeling almost intimidated by their intelligence. Well beyond the little exercises I made them complete, they seemed to understand the world in a unique way.

Their intelligence, however, had its shortcomings. It was still difficult to leave them alone without supervision, even for a moment. I lived in constant fear of an accident. I had one eye on them at all times. At home and outside, I didn't stray more than a few metres from them. When I showered or went to the bathroom I left the door open so that I could hear what they were doing. The rule was that they weren't allowed to leave the floor of the house I was on, which they generally respected.

One day when they were about four years old, I was in the bathroom, door open, even though I was on my period. I turned to reach the drawer where I keep the tampons and when I turned back, I found the two of them standing in the doorway, watching me intensely.

"Boys, leave mommy alone, I'm on the toilet. I'm almost finished."

They didn't budge, and just kept staring. I sat motionless on the toilet, not knowing what to do. I told them again, this time angrily. But rather than obey, Vanya got down on his knees and tilted his head to get a better look.

Breathless, I inserted the tampon hastily, got dressed and shut myself in the bedroom. I sat for a long time on the bed, one hand over my mouth. I never wanted to come out. After that, I never again used the bathroom without locking the door, even to brush my teeth.

Another time, I woke up in the middle of the night and found them standing at the foot of the bed. They observed me wordlessly. I blinked a few times and tried to compose my thoughts. I should have asked them if something was wrong, if they'd had a nightmare or if they were sick, but I couldn't put the words together. I lay there naked, unable to pull myself from the bed. I could only look from one to the other. How long the scene lasted, I don't know. They finally went back to their room and I lay there, wondering if I'd dreamt it.

I never told Gregory about these incidents. I felt embarrassed and questioned whether I had somehow unknowingly provoked the situations. Had I not been modest enough? Had I not established limits? Guilt gnawed away at me and I didn't know what to feel guilty about. So I kept these shameful episodes a secret. The last thing I wanted to do was limit their curiosity.

TO CHANNEL THE BOYS' ENERGY, our schedule had become firm and structured: we had breakfast together, then, when Gregory left for work, I cleaned the kitchen while the boys dressed themselves. After that, we started our lessons. We worked four subjects for forty-five minutes every day. From 9:00 to 9:45, for example, we did math. At five years old, the boys could already add and subtract, as well as solve simple problems. From 9:45 to 10:30, we did French; they were gradually learning to read and write, with a focus on encyclopedic texts rather than fiction, which didn't interest them at all. Then they had a break. I let them play for thirty minutes, or we would go for a walk outside. From 11:00 to 11:45 we would start back up with science; we looked at insects or soil through a magnifying glass, studied the reaction of vinegar with baking soda, or chose an animal to research. Finally, from 11:45 to 12:30 we did what I liked to call philosophy; this was where we got to talk about emotions, people, the environment, religion... Following that, they got another play period while I prepared lunch, and then we went on an outing. The days were full, but this system worked well. I wouldn't say they were avid learners—they didn't ask many questions or take much initiative—but they listened and learned easily. The lessons significantly reduced their aggression.

At the end of the first year, the Toronto District School Board required that home-schooled children take a general exam to make sure they were meeting Ontario program requirements. I had no doubt that the twins would pass effortlessly.

The exam was scheduled on a Friday at the neighbourhood school's gym. That morning, I hadn't bothered to explain to the boys why we were going to the school, as I wanted to avoid causing them any undue stress. I simply dressed them nicely and did their hair, and we set out.

I had imagined that the board had chosen this date because there was a school holiday, and was surprised to discover that it was in fact a day like any other and the school was full of children. A sign pointed us to the gym, where we were greeted by the elementary school principal. In the gym, they had set out little tables, on which were placed a few sheets of paper, a pencil, and an eraser. A number of children would be completing the mandatory exam at the same time. We waited on the stage for the rest of the little candidates to arrive. There was a dozen. I was stunned that this many children in the neighbourhood were home-schooled. I thought we were the only ones. The twins examined every child who walked into the gym. It was obvious that many of them had learning disabilities, which explained their parents' choice.

The exam was made up of a written component, which tested a number of school subjects, and an oral exam, during which each child met individually with a teacher. The whole thing happened in the gym, with the interviews held in a secluded corner. It took about an hour to complete the two parts of the exam, at the end of which we went home. The results would be mailed to us.

On the way home, the twins refused to walk beside me,

preferring to trail behind. On the doorstep, they stopped and wouldn't go into the house. They refused together as one.

"What are you doing? Come on," I said.

"No," replied Vanya.

"Do you want to play outside?" I asked.

"No," replied Daniil.

"What's going on? Are you upset?"

"It's over," said Vanya after a pause.

"What's over, Vanya?" I asked, starting to lose patience.

"We don't want to work here anymore. We want to go to school."

It felt like I was the one who had just failed the exam.

Because it was the children's decision, Gregory was remarkably conciliatory.

"It's a good thing that they want to be with others. You must have boosted their confidence and now they're ready."

I wondered whether they were more interested in escaping me than integrating, but I kept that thought to myself.

And so it was that, in September, once I had performed all the necessary steps, they went straight into grade two. They would soon be seven years old. The administration insisted on placing them in separate classes; it was the policy for all children from the same family, they told me, to put an end to my protestations.

I delayed my return to work for a few more weeks. I needed to make sure the children were adapting well to their new school setting. One day I decided to go in anyway, just to regain my bearings. I spent the whole morning wandering the hallways of our company, repeating the same phrases on a loop to anyone who asked, without immersing myself in any of the projects suggested to me. My head was empty. I had forgotten how to do my job. After wasting the whole morning, I went down to the coffee maker. Two young colleagues whose names I didn't know were just finishing their cappuccinos, standing at the high tables. I gave them a quick wave before making my selection on the machine. With my little cup in hand, I hesitated to join them. I told myself it was the thing to do, but didn't really want to. Lacking the courage to feign interest in them, I smiled politely at them and left.

"That's her: Gregory's wife."

I hadn't fully turned the corner, but they couldn't see me. I flattened myself against the wall and waited for them to continue.

"Is she older than him?"

"I don't know... Dave told me I was going to have to show her how to use Revit, because it turns out she only knows AutoCAD."

"What is she supposed to work on if she can't use the software?"

"On whatever she wants, I suppose. She is the boss, after all, like Greg."

"That's crazy, when I've been here three years and they still only assign me the shit projects."

I spent the afternoon holed up in my office, rolling my chair between the drawing table and the computer. At two-thirty, I escaped to go pick the boys up from school. The firm that bore my name no longer belonged to me.

"Oh, you're Vanya's mom, right? I'd like to have a word with you."

In a friendly but firm gesture, the teacher took me aside. "We had a little incident... It seems Vanya was inspecting another boy's anus."

That was the word she used: "anus." It seemed as strange to me as my son's actions.

"But why would he do that?" I spoke to the teacher, but watched Vanya, who stood casually beside me.

"I don't know. The other little boy complained afterwards that Vanya had looked at his private parts."

Anus, private parts. The vocabulary embarrassed me as much as the situation.

"Has he ever been to a psychologist?"

I gritted my teeth. The teacher asked me to have a talk with Vanya to make sure it never happened again.

"Were you curious? Did you want to see if he was made like you? Did you touch it?"

On the walk home, I tried to get some clarity on what had happened, but Vanya didn't seem to understand my questions. The day was grey and cool and I had forgotten his coat at school. Vanya held Daniil's hand as they walked. I changed my tone, trying to make him understand the gravity of the situation: "That's not right, Vanya, you can't undress your friends."

"He's not my friend."

I dropped my shoulders. "But why did you look at his bum?"

Vanya hesitated, appearing to think this time. "I wanted to see if he tasted like Daniil."

He turned, smiling, toward his brother, as I stopped in my tracks, paralyzed on the sidewalk. The twins passed me as they continued toward the house. I didn't want an explanation. I didn't want to know.

"All kids fool around like that," said Gregory sharply when I told him the story.

"If that was the case, the school wouldn't have recommended a psychologist."

"Listen, it's very clearly an attempt to get your attention. Even though they're at school, the boys still need you."

"You think they're doing this because I went back to work?" Despite everything, it was a relief to think they needed me.

"Emma, I think your place is at home now. You'll remain a full partner, of course."

He negotiated, but it wasn't necessary. He didn't need to convince me; I had relinquished my career over five years ago, and the mourning period was long since over. The prospect of being a stay-at-home mom suited me perfectly, in the grand scheme of things.

When I found a note in their bags the next day, I was sure it was another problem. Instead, it was a permission slip for a trip to the Royal Ontario Museum. The school was looking for parents to volunteer to accompany the classes. I was happy to be able to participate in the outing. We had a family membership, and had often gone to see the dinosaur skeletons on our afternoon excursions. I'd read them the signs and they'd play question games on the touch screen. A single room could occupy us for hours.

The morning of the trip, I dressed the boys in bright colours in order to be able to find them easily in the crowd of children, something I did whenever we went out like this.

In the schoolyard, the children waited excitedly. The activity combined the two second-grade classes, making sixty children and six adults, including the parent volunteers. We would take the subway.

They had put me in charge of a group of ten children, mostly boys. Watching them run down the escalators and step dangerously close to the subway trains, I wondered if the school hadn't assigned me the most difficult ones. Or did I just have no authority over children?

The trip consisted mainly of a series of routines: snack, bathroom, lunch, snack, bathroom. The twins had learned so much more during our visits. The whole outing seemed like such a waste of time compared to my lessons. For the moment, my main concern was avoiding disruptions, especially by one of my children. Easily identifiable by their red and yellow shirts, Vanya and Daniil were fairly well behaved through the tour. A trip through the games room concluded the visit. We warmly thanked the girl who had acted as our guide and the group prepared to head back to school.

We were all jammed into the subway tunnel. It was nearly three o'clock and the stop was packed. I frantically scanned my group of children, trying to keep them all in a line. That's when I lost sight of the twins. In a panic, I looked up and down the platform. How could they have escaped my view? I ordered my group to hold hands and backed them against a pillar, so I could step away for a moment to look for the twins. I saw them right away, on the upper floor, coming out of the public washroom.

"What are you doing? Come down here right now."

"Daniil had to pee," said Vanya.

"You can't walk away like that. Get down here and get in line with the others."

With a hand on my heart, I tried to calm down. We were about to step on the train when a teacher ordered us to stop.

We were missing a child.

Someone set off the alarm and the loudspeakers began to blare an insistent tone to alert us to the emergency. The children were running every which way and couldn't hear what I was screaming to them. I caught a few of them and held them firmly against a wall. With my arms extended, I created a barrier to protect my ten children. I tried to follow what was happening, but there was such chaos in the station that I didn't know where the danger was coming from. They had stopped the subway, and every train and platform was being searched at a frantic pace by a teacher and TTC security staff. Twenty minutes passed before the police and fire department were alerted to what the media would quickly label "the disappearance of little Faye."

Dozens of help staff flew past, shouting contradictory orders: some told us to stay put, while others shoved us around, telling us to move. Cornered by a staircase, I couldn't see the other groups from the school.

The adults' worry quickly took hold of the children, who were getting harder and harder to control. Some sobbed, while others became hyperactive or catatonic. I got my group to sit against the wall. One of the children was about to faint. In no way concerned like the others, the twins stayed calm and watched the comings and goings like it was a circus.

"We have to evacuate," declared an agent after more than two hours of searching. "Start taking down everyone's contact information before they leave. And round up the whole school group and bring them to the station."

Seeing the police vans, the children began jostling each other excitedly for a place in the back seat. They arrived gleefully at the station, as though they were getting off a merry-go-round.

During the individual interviews, the police determined that at the time of her disappearance, seven-year-old Faye was wearing a grey fleece, a flowered T-shirt, white canvas pants, and sneakers. Her school photo appeared everywhere: a little blond girl with a proud, gap-toothed smile. In September, the twins had had a photo taken in front of the same fake library backdrop.

She had most likely last been seen at the entrance to the Museum subway station. The teacher assured the investigators that was where she had last counted the children, but she had no specific memory of having seen Faye. This information would be repeated in the media during the two weeks the Amber Alert lasted.

They asked for help from the public to find the girl, and I immediately volunteered to participate in the search. School started back up after a day of debriefing, and I needed to be involved. I felt responsible, even if I hadn't been the one looking after the child.

The search units met at Queen's Park, close to the site of Faye's disappearance. As soon as I'd dropped the boys off at school, I walked to the meeting place. It was October, but it was warm out. I had put on sneakers and a light scarf with a Marc Jacobs tweed coat.

I fought back a burst of joy when I spotted Oliver among the crowd of volunteers. It had been a long time since I'd seen him. We waved from afar as we listened to the police instructions. They told us to scour the area, establishing a large perimetre around the subway station. Police officers interrogated the neighbouring merchants and a few residents, but the area around Queen's Park mainly consisted of stores, hospitals, and University of Toronto buildings.

The volunteers followed a very strict procedure. In groups of seven, we were to inspect the ground in a precise location, paying attention to any detail that looked like it could be linked to the disappearance—scraps of cloth, objects, debris, traces of blood. Arm in arm, we walked in step, examining the ground. The possibility of finding something horrified me, but I also wanted to do a good job. Oliver hurried over to join my group. When I hooked my arm in his, a shiver went down my spine. His elbow was warm and I could smell the laundry detergent from his clothes. From the corner of my eye I watched him move his feet carefully over the ground. I was suddenly overcome by the fluttering of my heart.

"Are you okay, Emma?" he asked, furrowing his brow.

I couldn't answer. I let go of his elbow and slipped away from the group. I was here to find a little girl who might be dead, and I was flirting.

I pretended to check my phone before announcing that I had to go. Jerkily, almost running, I fled the investigation site.

As I turned onto Harbord Street, I leaned against a tree some distance from the sidewalk to catch my breath. With my face in my hands, I tried to control my tears. My back slid down the tree trunk and I found myself sitting in the dirty gravel. I let my fingers drag through the rocks, trying to catch my breath. I picked a sharp one. The stone was not sharp enough to cut through the skin of my wrist, but I scratched myself a few times until the pain relieved me.

When I finally opened my eyes, I realized that a student had stopped and was watching me. He opened his mouth, but stopped himself before turning and resuming his path. I dusted off my clothes and hurried home.

That night, while watching the news on CBC, I learned the searches had turned up nothing. Faye had vanished into thin air. I received a text from Oliver, which I decided to ignore—along with the barrage of them he sent after.

The Amber Alert was lifted a few days later; the police declared that little Faye would not be found alive. The evidence leading them to this conclusion was not revealed to the media. The only thing left to do was forget.

Forget.

PART TWO

"YOU'VE GOT A SKIN FOLD ON YOUR WAIST THERE."

"I know."

"You need to get rid of it."

"Well, what about your pectorals? Why aren't they developing?"

"I told you, it's because my rib cage isn't as big as yours."

"You have to work your upper body more."

Our regimen has been effective. Our muscles are bulging and defined. Before we begin, we take the scale from under the bed and weigh ourselves. We are respectively 156 and 159 pounds. Our BMI is 21.7 and 22; we can calculate this mentally.

We perform a series of stretches and head to the park. It isn't far; it's the one at our old elementary school. We still spend a lot of time there. In the afternoon, it fills up with children who watch us exercise and try to make fun by imitating us. We don't care.

"You have to get your chin over the bar."

"You're not even getting there yourself!"

"You have to if we're going to have the same pectorals."

At opposite ends of the bars, we coordinate the rhythm of our lifts. We do two hundred, breathing together as one. The symmetry has to be perfect. Next, we do sprints: forty times across the park, then two hundred squats.

When we finish training, we buy Gatorade at the convenience store on Harbord Street.

"Are we going to the dog park to drink them?"

A dry grass covers the clearing and prickles our thighs through our shorts. A man and woman are talking while their dogs run around them. We watch them as we drink our Gatorade. A boy passes us with a big grey dog. The beast comes over to sniff us, and the boy gives a tug on his leash. The dog circles the park a few times before shitting in a corner. The boy picks it up, lets the dog play for a bit, then climbs the hill to leave the park.

"What kind of dog is that?"

We like dogs.

"A poodle," the boy responds flatly.

"A poodle. He doesn't look like a poodle."

"That's because people usually shave them into stupid shapes."

The dog sits down. No one pets him. A moment passes.

"Do you want to come to the pool with us? We're going to Christie Pits," we ask before getting up to go.

The boy accepts right away. We don't really know why we asked him.

"I'll get my bathing suit at home and meet you there."

"Should we try the five-metre?"

We put our clothes away in lockers. The keys hang from our wrists on rubber bands.

The pool is made up of four areas. The first, very shallow, has a shower shaped like a mushroom for babies, but the water is so cold you can't stay in there long. The second is too hot. If you jump into it first, the last two pools feel like ice. The bigger, main one is Olympic size and we can usually get in a few laps of front crawl when it isn't overrun by amateur swimmers. The last one is just the landing pool for the diving boards; this is the one we like best. Boys perform ridiculous feats for the sake of the girls in bikinis lying out on their towels.

There are four incrementally higher diving boards: two small one-metre ones, the three-metre above them, and the five-metre platform dominating the tower.

Our towels are sitting off to the side. They are different colours and our names are embroidered on them in capital letters. Someone made a comment about them one time. But he knows better now.

We climb the steps and take position at the edge of the platform. We are the only divers on top of the tower, so we can take our time. A lifeguard is stationed nearby to authorize the jump. He is fat and tanned. He gives us a sidelong glance, no smile.

"You can go," he says dully.

We look at the tips of our feet and a point in the water where we will land. Without hesitation, we propel ourselves forward as far as possible, before curving our body to form as perfect a vertical position as we can. We pierce the water with minimal splash around the point of impact. We smile discreetly.

"Not bad."

The boy with the poodle is waiting at the side of the pool.

"Can you dive off the five-metre?"

"No, but I can jump," he says.

"Let's go."

The three of us climb to the top of the tower. We signal to the boy that he has to go first. He positions himself, toes hooked over the concrete, at the very edge of the diving board.

"Go ahead," says the lifeguard, yawning.

The boy doesn't budge. He looks into the void, then back at us. We cross our arms at the same time. He resumes his position, hesitates again, bends his knees into a squat, leans forward a little, and jumps. We lean over the guardrail to watch him land. His feet and thighs smack the water. He swims to the side with his head out of the water.

All afternoon, we dive, concentrating primarily on the 101A, the 203C, and the 5122D. The boy is happy to keep jumping.

We show him how to perfect his crawl. He is a fast learner. He follows our rhythm unquestioningly and stops when we tell him it is time to leave. He watches as we walk away. We tell him not to follow us.

"How old would you say he is?"

"I don't know. Ten? Eleven, maybe?"

THE TWINS HAD DEVELOPED MAGNIFICENTLY; they were huge, athletic, dark despite their blondness, exactly the kind of boys I was crazy for when I was a teenager. At nearly sixteen, they still did everything together.

Earlier that year, we made some major renovations to the house and offered them their own rooms. Gregory suggested building an addition to the house to make some extra space. He spent days working on the plans, with an eye to the strict zoning laws in the neighbourhood, but the boys refused outright. So I limited myself to updating the decor. The walls, originally blue, were repainted in grey tones to match their new bedding. A set of deer antlers replaced the colourful bunting, and the carpet adorned with dancing monkeys made way for a thicker new one, with a triangular pattern. But I was proudest of having snagged them authentic Peter Løvig Nielsen desks—two 1958 Boomerang-Schreibtischs in perfect condition.

But the desks didn't get much use. The boys didn't spend much time studying. Their academic performance was, in fact, not very good. Their childhood passions, biology, nature, animals, had dwindled. Gregory assured me there was nothing to worry about; I think he hoped that their mediocre grades would make them one day turn to us for jobs at the firm.

At the end of the school year, their marks in English were so weak that their teacher suggested summer courses. They had no command of the basics and in his opinion, if no action was taken, the gap would only widen and they risked failing in their final year.

"It would be a shame to make them miss out on their summer," I said. "I think they could use a break. I can take care of catching them up—I taught them when they were young, after all. Besides, anyone can teach literature, right?"

Gregory agreed. We remained suspicious of the school system, which had so often misjudged the boys. Gregory would be travelling for a large part of the summer, which had become the norm. He spent nearly half the year on the road. To some extent, it's what had allowed our relationship to survive over the years where a number of our friends had divorced—among them, Magalie, who had moved to Vancouver some time ago. When Gregory worked on a contract abroad, I followed my own schedule. When he returned, we were glad to see each other. It had taken me some time to accept this system, but I'd come to see it only as a good thing.

That morning, I sat the twins down at the kitchen table and presented them the list of books I wanted them to read over the summer. I decided to start with Alice Munro, because she'd won the Nobel Prize for Literature the previous fall. I'd never read her myself, but I was planning to discover her alongside the boys. Shortly after, they'd left for Robarts Library to borrow the books, and I was now waiting for them to return.

They wasted no time coming home—empty-handed.

"What? You were supposed to go to the library. What did you do?"

"We went diving."

"You're diving again?" The notion moved me. They hadn't dived in nearly four years, since the accident.

I had discovered their interest in diving when they were around eight. I often took them to the pool when they were little and was the one who taught them to swim. It was impossible to sign them up for swimming lessons. I tried once, but they were always escaping the teacher's supervision and I spent the whole lesson worrying they would drown. I wasn't a strong swimmer myself, but I was good enough to be able to teach them the basics of the front crawl and breaststroke. They had learned to imitate me and had quickly become better swimmers than I was. Around that time, they started watching YouTube videos and asking me to film them. They didn't want me in the pool with them; it wasn't necessary because they were such good swimmers. They wanted me to film them while they swam so that they could perfect their moves, like the professionals.

I had to negotiate permission with the pool staff, because filming generally wasn't permitted at the pool. I was only allowed to film when they were alone in the water, which meant we started visiting the pool earlier and earlier in the morning. At six o'clock the pool was free, so for a number of months they asked to go swimming before school in order for me to film them. Later, they'd compare their performance to the professionals and would work together to improve. I imagine it was through following links on YouTube that they came across diving videos, because one day they told me they didn't want to swim anymore; they wanted to dive.

The neighbourhood pool didn't have a diving board, but the University of Toronto offered children's diving classes. We signed them up for classes and they were noticed right away. For one thing, their swimming style was impeccable, but most notably, unlike the other children starting out in diving, they had no fear. While the others stood with their feet glued to the edge of the platform, the twins flung themselves into the void without hesitation, indifferent to the pain if they made a flat landing.

After the course's first session, the instructor approached me to ask whether they would be interested in joining the competitive team. It was a big commitment because the schedules were so demanding. The team trained four weekdays from six to eight in the morning, with tournaments on weekends. But it was a period when Gregory was away, so it was easy for me to adapt to the program.

For over three years, diving consumed their lives. As a result, it consumed mine too. I woke up in the wee hours to make them a first breakfast, a light but energy-packed snack, and then I drove them to the university pool. From the bleachers, I watched them train for two hours. Then I brought them home and made them a second breakfast before taking them to school. When I picked them up at the end of the day, they talked of nothing but points, somersaults, spins, and rotations. The moment they got home, they went straight to the computer and studied the videos of the champions, then shut themselves in their room to do stretching and strengthening exercises. On weekends, I accompanied them to competitions across the region, which quickly became competitions all across Ontario. Gregory tried to come with us when he was around. When he wasn't, he followed their performances through the videos I sent him.

I saw the same parents from one competition to the next, particularly the mothers. We exchanged a few words. Our stories were similar; our children fuelled by the same passion. Some parents were even former divers themselves and showed no restraint in shouting direction from the bleachers. Competition days were long. I generally took a magazine and some hand creams to keep myself busy between events. The twins never came to sit with me, preferring to stay together at the side of the pool when others performed. I watched them engage in critical, concentrated discussion of the other competitors' execution.

One Saturday, we were in Kitchener for the regional championships, and the boys were waiting for their second turn. They had done well on their first dive and were up for the semi-final. I was concentrating on reading *Garden Design* when I felt a hand on my shoulder. It was a woman in her forties, with greying hair, dressed for a yoga class.

"You're the twins' mother, aren't you?"

I didn't know her.

"I remember you," she said. "We met at an APAR meeting. I'm Marie."

I nodded, still embarrassed at the recollection of the assault.

"So your children are diving now."

"Yes, they're with Dive Toronto." I pointed to the boys, sitting together in their uniforms, their long hair spilling down their backs.

"My daughter dives too," she said.

This woman was making me uncomfortable. I remembered her now; she was the mother who already had a biological daughter and had adopted a baby from Russia after that. Her hair was brown back then. I had nothing to say to her, but she seemed in a mood to pursue the conversation.

"How are things with your boys?"

"Good. And with your son?"

"Alexei is in foster care five days a week. His autism has become unmanageable, and we were eligible for relief care funding."

"He doesn't live with you?" I closed my magazine.

"Only on the weekends. We decided it was best for him and for our daughter."

So they rejected the adopted child in favour of the biological one? I couldn't conceal my frown. The mother looked off into the distance and said nothing else. I brought my attention back to the pool, where the competition continued.

The twins were now in the line for the three-metre board. They had to execute a 401C. Daniil went first. His tuck looked perfect to me, but the movement was a little too slow and he was still angled when he hit the water. I watched Vanya close his eyes and react along with him. Then Vanya energetically climbed the steps for his turn, assumed his position, back facing the pool, heels at the very edge of the platform, arms perfectly extended. His jump was explosive and his tuck very high, allowing him to establish a perfect vertical, winning him the Most Promising title for the region.

At first, I thought the competition would create rivalry between the boys, but Daniil seemed as satisfied with the accomplishments of Vanya as his own, and vice versa. Even their way of speaking reflected this reciprocity; they never said "I won the title," but "we won the title." I was impressed by their team spirit.

"Congratulations," said Marie before leaving the sports complex. Her voice carried a twinge of regret.

I was astounded when the twins announced that, three years after stopping, they'd gone diving. I forgot I had to do something about the Munro books they hadn't gone to pick up. "Where did you go?"

"To the pool at Christie Pits."

Daniil shot Vanya a look, as though he wanted him to shut up. Christie Pits was a poorly equipped, poorly maintained municipal pool. The university athletic centre where

126

they'd trained until they were eleven was on Spadina Avenue, where the facilities were much more luxurious and appropriate for diving. They didn't have access anymore, since it was a private pool. The Dive Toronto team was very disappointed to lose two of its greatest hopes, but the penalty was permanent. The offence had been too great.

It happened in 2010, during the national competition. Toronto was hosting, and the boys would be competing in their own pool, giving them the home advantage. Their trainer, Marc, had put a lot of pressure on them because he knew there was a chance they'd take the gold. The month before, he had gone so far as to double their number of training sessions; the boys had to show up at the pool after school as well. The stakes were so high that Gregory had cancelled a trip to Germany in order to watch the competition.

But the day before, Jules had disappeared. I noticed when he didn't show up for his morning kibble. He was an indoor cat and he was old. I worried about him getting outside. The twins had to attend a final training session, and I explained to them that I would drop them off and come back to look for Jules with Gregory during their lesson.

Searching for the cat with increasing concern, I told myself that the boys must have misjudged the severity of the situation, remembering how casually they'd left for training. I searched the flowerbeds, crawled under the porches, calling his name as though he could answer me. It was Gregory who finally found him.

"Emma—he's here."

Gregory was at the end of the road, crouching in a flowered shrub. He had taken off his sweater and was trying to put the cat in it. I didn't see Jules in the fabric.

"Is he dead?" I asked as I approached him.

"No… not yet."

I held off looking into Gregory's arms until the last possible moment. The cat's neck was all soft and his head was tilted at an absurd angle. Gregory had swaddled him like a baby.

"His… his tail is gone," he said in a sob.

I looked at him, uncomprehending. "What do you mean his tail is gone?" I scanned the garment hiding Jules's body.

"Come on."

We walked to the house. Gregory set Jules on the armchair in the living room and gently opened the sweater protecting him. Jules breathed deeply, his whole body shaken with the effort. His fur was coarse and fluffy, and his back now ended in a tiny appendage—a little tail a few centimetres long.

"But what was he doing outside? Why did he go out? Did he get hit?"

I wanted to accuse the cat of his stupidity, to punish him. Gregory was equally baffled.

"I don't think so."

"Was he attacked by a raccoon?"

Raccoon attacks were common in Toronto. Any number of cats and even dogs were regularly wounded when they found themselves in the path of these wild, overly familiar beasts. Gregory turned toward me, really crying now. It was his cat.

"Emma, he's been mutilated… someone cut off his tail. The wound is clean."

A horrible thought occurred to me, but I chased it away. Jules was in agony. We couldn't leave him in this state.

"We have to get him to the vet."

"What time is it?"

We had to pick the boys up at the pool. And we had only one car.

"Take Jules, I'll drop you at the vet and go get the boys. We'll call afterward to figure out what to do."

Gregory nodded his head, glad I was taking control of things. He wrapped Jules back up, holding him close, and we left.

I didn't even have time to park at the athletic centre before Gregory called.

"Emma? They had to put him down."

I rubbed the corners of my eyes as I hung up. When the twins came out of the locker room, I'd already prepared my speech.

"Boys, I have some bad news."

I paused to let the announcement sink in. They looked up at me, waiting.

"It's Jules. We found him, but he was very hurt. Daddy had to take him to the vet, and he's gone to sleep forever."

Then something very strange happened. The boys, without even looking at each other, smiled at me with a softness, a gentleness I had never seen in them. It was a simple, natural smile, delicately closing their eyes, bringing out their cheeks, pink from sport. I stood for a moment amazed by the radiance I had never seen on their faces. They smiled without irony or malice, but like normal children.

My shoulders sank. I didn't know what to do. "Come on, let's go get Daddy."

"Okay," said the boys, shaking their backpacks.

The next day, the first day of the competition, we left them to get ready, telling them over and over how proud we were of them, no matter what the outcome. They nodded before disappearing into the locker room. We hurried to the stands, which were already packed. All the competitors were grouped by team under their banners, which were hung on the wall beside the pool. The twins were late to join their team and I could see Marc, like me, scanning the crowd for them. When the judges took their positions, the boys still weren't there. The trainer went to the locker room. I was about to get up, but Gregory assured me Marc had things under control. Indeed, he appeared a few moments later, accompanied by the twins in uniform, and a boy from another team. The boy, in a red swimsuit, hurried to join his group and the boys to theirs, amid Marc's reprimands.

The competition was supposed to last the whole day. When the boys' turns came, I squeezed Gregory's hand, happy he was there to support them. The boys had prepared six dives: 101A, 203C, 302B, 401C, 5132D and 624C. They wouldn't necessarily have to execute them all. It would depend on the number of events they qualified for.

They only completed four—perfectly, at that.

For the 624C, the diver starts off standing on his hands before performing a twist. The boys had recently learned to walk on their hands precisely to master this difficult manoeuvre. When the boy in the red bathing suit appeared, trembling, on the five-metre board, the crowd realized something wasn't right. With his arms wrapped around his body, he was slow getting into position. He finally approached the edge of the platform, leaned over to put his weight on his hands, and lifted his body, one leg at a time, slowly and cautiously. He took a long time getting into the pose. In the bleachers, we held our breath. Despite the echo, the pool was quiet. I heard a long whistle. Then came the accident.

The boy's arms shook, unable to support his weight any longer. We heard the crack when his head hit the platform's concrete edge. His body collapsed before plunging into the emptiness and smacking against the water.

All at once the parents rose, shouting, while the trainers rushed into the pool to recover the boy. I didn't see them take him out on a stretcher, as I was already running toward the stairs. All the parents were trying to get to their children at the edge of the pool, but the trainers wouldn't let them pass.

They divided themselves up quickly and got the competitors dressed before returning our children to us, calling their names one by one. In the hall of the athletic centre, no one wanted to leave. Several families waited, us among them, to see how the boy was doing. Gregory had put an arm around each of the boys and kept them close at his sides.

"It's all right boys, he's in good hands. The ambulance is coming."

It took only a few minutes for the paramedics to come running at top speed. The crowd of families watched as the boy was briskly lifted onto a stretcher, a brace around his neck.

"They didn't put him on the respirator. That's a good sign. It means he can breathe on his own," Gregory pointed out to reassure the twins.

We returned home in a daze. Overloaded.

Later in the afternoon, we got a call from Marc, asking if he could come to the house to discuss something with us. He arrived a few hours later, accompanied by a police officer. At first, I couldn't understand why.

"I'd like to talk to you alone, please," he said.

I was sure he was going to tell us the boy was dead, and I pushed the twins into their room.

"Mateo is paralyzed," he began.

I covered my mouth with my hand. Gregory stood at my side, arms crossed, nodding sadly.

"He may never walk again."

"Oh, that's terrible," I said, my eyes filling with tears.

"Yes. He regained consciousness, but he's in a lot of pain. SickKids Hospital contacted me because he woke up talking about the twins.

"Our twins?" asked Gregory.

The police officer cleared his throat and this time, he was the one who spoke. "He said they scared him in the locker room, and that's why he fell."

I stopped breathing for a moment. Gregory was already on the defensive.

"Well come on, why would he say that? It's not as though they pushed him."

"Calm down, sir. I'm here to tell you that we're investigating this as a case of severe intimidation. Mateo said that your children shamed him physically and threatened him."

"How did they threaten him?" Gregory flung his arms as he spoke.

"Your sons told him that they could put a curse on him... Did you hear a whistle at the pool?"

Yes, I thought.

"No," said Gregory.

"According to Mateo, the twins hexed him by whistling to make him miss his dive."

"Oh come on, and you believe this nonsense?"

"Of course not. That's why I told you it was intimidation, and not witchcraft. I'd like to talk to Daniil and Vanya now."

"In the meantime," Marc said apologetically, "the boys are suspended from the club."

"But—" I looked from Marc to the policeman "—it's because they lost their cat yesterday."

I didn't know what I was saying anymore, so I stopped talking.

The twins' guilt could never be proven. It was the word of one against another. Regardless, because of pressure from other parents, Dive Toronto decided not to let the boys back onto the team.

They hadn't dived since. And we never got another cat.

I didn't know what to think about their sudden renewed interest in diving.

JULY WAS HOT BUT GREY THIS YEAR. Despite all the attention I lavished on my fig tree, I realized hopelessly that it wasn't growing. I had begun tearing out the invasive mint to make sure the roots weren't strangling the little fruit tree. I threw myself into the work for a good ten minutes before realizing I'd need a tool to complete the purge.

The garden shed was a mess, despite my best efforts. Unsurprisingly, my pruning shears weren't in their usual spot. I resigned myself to the fact that I was going to have to tidy up the shed if I was ever going to find them.

The children's toys still cluttered the lower shelves, and I figured it was time to organize the mess. I unrolled a clear recycling bag and started to fill it. Balls and plastic trucks gradually accumulated inside. The twins had never really played with those things.

Watching the toys pile up in the bag, I couldn't hold back a few silent tears. I remembered buying them, looking forward to the pleasure they would bring my children, but not one of these toys had interested them.

"What are you doing?"

Vanya stood before me. I hadn't heard him come in.

"Just a little cleaning," I said, sniffling discreetly.

He nodded with approval.

I held out my hand. "Do you need something, my love?"

He ignored my hand, which hung for a moment, suspended in the air, grotesque. Vanya turned and left without another word. His gait was supple, his body moving gracefully. His grey T-shirt stretched between his shoulders in a wide fold that fell down his lean back. On the nape of his neck, his hair had darkened and started to curl. He had no beard yet, but we guessed it would be the same deep blond. I thought he was so beautiful. And, then, the thought: I had no part in it.

The bag of toys yawned open before me. I closed it by tying the ends, not yet knowing what I wanted to do with it. I moved a few bags of soil, and finally saw the pruning shears in the back corner of a shelf. I had to contort myself to pull them out. Catching hold of the handles at last, I suddenly froze. There were traces of dried blood on the blades. When I touched it, part of the stain peeled off in a little strip. Who could have hurt themselves with them? I dropped the shears in disgust. I didn't feel like gardening anymore.

"Do you know their friend?" asked Gregory when he got home that night.

"What friend?"

"I just ran into the twins and they said they were going to play soccer in the empty lot with a friend."

I didn't know them to have a single friend. Any friendship they developed could only be a good thing, we figured.

"By the way, did you hurt yourself with the pruning shears?" I asked after a moment.

Gregory rarely did any gardening, as he usually took care of the larger construction or repair work.

"I found blood on them."

I'd spoken calmly, but Gregory became agitated right away.

"You found blood?"

I went to get the shears. There were only a few fine red streaks, but they covered about three quarters of the blade.

"I scratched off part of it with my nail," I said. "There was more before."

Gregory examined them, raised his eyebrows, and slammed them onto the table.

"I hope you haven't started again." His voice was hard.

"No," I said meekly. "I wanted to cut the mint stems."

There was no sense in explaining it.

"You're still taking your Cipralex?"

I confirmed in a tiny voice. Just after Faye's disappearance, Gregory discovered I was cutting myself again, and considered it an affront. I'd had serious episodes as a teenager, from which I still had scars on my arms. Gregory believed it was thanks to him that I'd stopped. He was partly right.

Stressing that I had everything I needed to be happy, that the children depended on me now and I couldn't let myself go down that road again, he'd stepped in and had our family doctor prescribe me antidepressants. I had to start taking care of myself. Our family's well-being depended on my mental health, he'd declared.

The drugs worked. I felt more at peace, but I had gained weight. I now tried to hide my ample form under loose clothes, preferably made of natural linen.

I was hurt by Gregory's accusation. How could he doubt me? I abandoned the pruning shears and tried to change the subject.

"The twins have taken up diving again."

Gregory instantly forgot the shears.

"THERE IT IS." We lay down our bikes in the grass and cross the vacant lot to the silo.

Twenty feet high and about fifteen feet wide, the tower must have been used to store grain, since the lot was agricultural land. The silo is made of cement and topped with a round metal dome, painted white. A ladder stretches up one side, providing access to a door in the roof. A metal tube descends from the same point. We don't know what it could be for. The structure is neglected; the cement is crumbling and the metal has rusted through. The ladder was cut off three metres from the ground, making it impossible to climb. We know because we've tried unsuccessfully to reach it.

We pull a dirty sports bag out from the high grass growing around the foot of the silo. We found it yesterday. We look around to make sure we're still alone. The bag contains a shredded rope, a rock-climbing hammer that's missing part of its handle, some old sneakers, and a wad of bills. We set it all out on the grass.

"How much is there?"

"A hundred and thirty dollars."

We'll decide later what to do with the money. First, we want to try the climbing tool. We didn't have time yesterday on our way back from the pool, because it was starting to get dark. Maybe we'll finally be able to reach the door.

The object, a sort of hybrid between a hammer and a saw, should help with the climb. But it's in bad shape with an uncertain grip. We try to drive it into the silo. The impact chips the concrete surface, but doesn't stick.

"We'll have to find cracks, rather than trying to cut holes."

We walk around the silo, examining the surface below the ladder. By planting the hammer in the concrete divots, we get enough hold to ensure a slow climb. The tool is heavier than we'd thought and is oddly shaped, which makes it hard to use. When we finally get purchase with it in the concrete, we have to pull hard to dislodge it and plant it higher. We nearly lose our balance every time. After several tries, we manage to climb a couple of metres up the smooth wall. We stretch our arms as wide as we can and look for a spot to brace our feet. The ladder is less than a metre above us. If we can bring our shoulders to the height of our hands, we will only have to reach an arm out to catch the first rung. But suddenly, the hammer slips under our weight and we fall back into the grass, getting the hammer right in the face. We worriedly examine the cut now opening up our chin. The wound is wide and open, but doesn't bleed much.

"You're going to need stitches."

We jump up. Standing behind us is what seems like a very thin boy with a hard look. His black-brown hair is shaved on one side and falls in long bangs on the other. He's wearing a plaid shirt, cut-off jean shorts, and black Converse sneakers.

"Are you sure?" We try to hide the panic in our voice.

"Yes. I got the same thing falling on skates," responds the teenager, lifting his head to reveal a long white scar on his hairless chin.

"I guess we'd better go home."

We get up unsteadily. We obviously can't pedal.

"I can take the other bike," the boy assures us.

"WHAT HAPPENED?"

Vanya staggered, holding his brother's arm, his chin bloodied.

"He fell," explained Daniil.

"Why are you weaving like that?" asked Gregory, moving closer.

"My back hurts," Vanya rasped.

Gregory gently lifted his T-shirt. Nearly his whole midsection was swollen in an enormous bruise.

"We've got to get him to the hospital right away," declared Gregory, already turning on his heels for the car keys.

I didn't say another word, and quickly stepped outside. At the foot of the porch steps stood a teenager holding Vanya's bike.

"Mathilde?" I hadn't seen Oliver's daughter in years, but I recognized her immediately. "What are you doing there?" I was asking questions with answers that didn't matter. I wanted to grab the bike and get in the car at the same time.

"I brought the bike back," Mathilde said simply. "I'll put it here." She took a few steps down the side alley and rested the bicycle against the wall of the house.

At SickKids, it didn't take long before we were seen. In less than an hour, they sewed up the cut on Vanya's chin and X-rayed his back. He had serious internal bleeding, so they decided to keep him under observation overnight. Despite Gregory's authority, the twins refused to tell us what happened.

"Vanya fell."

"Fell from where? Did you go diving again?"

"No. We just fell."

"Daniil, that's enough. I'm talking to Vanya. Vanya? We need to know what happened so that we can get you the appropriate treatment."

"I fell."

"Stop with this stupid game! Where were you?"

"Outside."

"Seriously, I've had enough of this. You're going to obey me and answer my questions this time!"

"He was outside, and he fell."

"Fuck, Daniil!"

"Gregory, please, I think they're tired."

I sat in the leather chair beside the bed and decided to spend the night there. Gregory had to go home alone with Daniil. It was already late, but Daniil refused to leave.

"He'll be home tomorrow," said Gregory, not knowing whether that was true.

Daniil hesitated. "I'll stay and you go home," he said, looking at me.

"That's impossible, Daniil. They won't let you be responsible for your brother."

He finally, reluctantly followed his father.

I looked at Vanya, spent, sound asleep despite himself. His features had softened and looked suddenly fragile and childlike. I stopped myself from caressing his pale cheek, concerned I might wake him, or disgust him. I contented myself with bringing my nose close to his face so I could smell his breath, like I'd done when he was a baby.

WE WAKE UP NAUSEOUS WITH A PASTY MOUTH. Our back doesn't hurt, as we're stuffed with medication. We want to touch the scar on our chin, but we can't feel anything under the bandage protecting the sutures. We turn our attention to Emma, asleep with her mouth open in the chair beside us.

The IV coming out of our hand aches with a kind of sickening pain. We don't dare move so as not to displace the needle, and we don't know what to do now that we're awake. What time is it? Sun is coming in through the window, but we wouldn't know if it was eight, noon, or two in the afternoon.

Emma stirs suddenly.

"How do you feel?" she asks, instantly worried.

"I'm okay."

She wants to touch our forehead, but we recoil.

"I'll let the doctor know you're awake," she announces, leaving the room.

The doctor has a guttural laugh that we hear from way down the hospital. Emma is standing with her arms crossed when Gregory arrives.

"He's a tough one. The hematoma is already healing and there are no complications. He can leave this afternoon, once he's downed one of our delicious meals and used the bathroom."

Turning toward us: "You understand what I explained to you? It's important to make sure that everything is working inside, eh?"

"Yes."

The doctor gives us a quick wave and walks out, his nose already in the next file.

"We'll leave you for a moment, boys. We're going to get a coffee," announces Gregory. "Do you want anything?"

"No."

Our grey night shirt smells like antiseptic. We have an unpleasant sense of déjà vu. Something about the atmosphere of this hospital makes us uncomfortable. The green walls are choking us. The odours are seeping in through all our pores. This hospital is haunting us. We need to leave. Right away.

As soon as we return to the house on Grace Street, we tell Gregory and Emma that we're going out. Gregory hesitates, looking us up and down. We're nearly as tall as him.

"I'll give you thirty minutes, only because the doctor said that walking would help the bruising to heal, but Vanya can't overdo it. No nonsense this time, okay?" he decides to add.

We head straight for the vacant lot. This time we survey the surroundings extra carefully to make sure the girl isn't there. We hunch over as we walk toward the silo, to make ourselves look smaller so we can pass unobserved. Digging in the grass, we find the bag right away, and make sure all our goods are still in there. They are.

"Are you going to give back my bag and my money?"

We jump! Where had she come from? We were looking over our shoulder the whole time and didn't see her coming.

Mathilde stands next to us, her arms resting beside her

thin body, her eyes planted on us. She has long eyelashes and a delicate mouth, but it's hard to see a girl in the hardened creature with the shaved hair.

"We don't have it." We're lying. To change the subject, we add, "What's all this for?"

Mathilde sits in the grass not far from us and scans the horizon. She explains that she spent a lot of time playing in the empty field when she was young and it became a kind of refuge. She's been fighting with her parents. She's planning to run away and stay here while she thinks of a solution.

"I know how to get in the door," she says, pointing her chin toward the sky.

A hollow appears between her collarbones, and her esophagus protrudes. It's this thinness that makes her look masculine.

"Can you show us how to climb up there?"

Mathilde smiles.

"Maybe."

She shoots us a dirty look.

"If you give me my money back... Plus forty dollars."

With this, she gets up, grabs her bag, and disappears into the woods surrounding the lot. We watch her as she goes. When she walks, the top of her body seems immobile under her oversized clothes.

"THEY DON'T RESPECT YOU, EMMA."

August was well underway, and the boys hadn't read a single one of the books I'd given to them. I insisted that the accident had upset our lessons, but Gregory didn't accept the excuse. He was just passing through Toronto and felt that things weren't going well in his absence. He worried now that I didn't have the authority to make sure the boys passed English.

I had to be tough. But making those two big young men obey me was not so easy. I was intimidated by their height, but nonetheless I couldn't let them dominate me. I was still their mother, after all.

I would mend our relationship by force. I ordered them to help me with the gardening chores—mowing the lawn, trimming the hedges—but I didn't want to ask too much of them so as not to tire Vanya, who was still recovering. The boys went obediently to work. It was a start.

While they worked, I watched them from the bay window in the kitchen. Gregory had settled into the living room with his iPad, but I got the impression he was evaluating me more than actually reading the news.

The twins' movements were quick and precise. Their tasks didn't occupy them for long. Next, I asked them to wash the windows. Sweaty and dirty, they came to see me in the kitchen when their work was done, leaving muddy tracks behind them.

"Come on, take off your shoes. Look, you're getting everything dirty."

They glanced indifferently at the mess and took off their shoes in silence.

"Socks too!" I added sharply, assuming Gregory was watching.

Their socks slid into a ball on the ground. It was then I noticed a dark spot under Vanya's foot.

"What's that tattoo?"

Gregory leapt from behind his screen. There was an inscription under Vanya's bare foot.

He resisted, trying to stop me from touching him, but my grip was firm. In blue ink, a word was written in an uncertain hand. The points were sloppy and the letters collapsed on themselves, making it hard to read. Vanya had obviously done the tattoo himself. Unless his brother had done it? I yelled at the boys to go to their room. I wanted to be alone with Gregory.

"Fe."

"It could be a brand, or a logo," Gregory guessed.

I suddenly wondered whether Daniil had also gotten a tattoo. Gregory's face dropped. We stormed into their room, the door hitting the wall.

The twins were stretched out together on Daniil's bed. Pressed tight to each other, they stared at the ceiling. Vanya hadn't bothered to put on other socks and in this position, his tattoo was clearly visible. How had I not seen it before?

"Daniil, do you have a tattoo as well?"

"Yes."

"Show me."

It was the same.

"Since when? What does it mean?"

My voice trembled. I nervously scratched the nape of my neck as I spoke. Each question I thought of led to another, which I didn't ask, knowing they wouldn't respond. I didn't know what to think anymore. I left their room, slamming the door.

"Listen, it's not that big a deal, Emma. I mean, I have the Budweiser logo on my shoulder, after all. It's just kids being kids."

GETTING FORTY DOLLARS ISN'T A PROBLEM. Our parents have been giving us an allowance that we don't know what to do with for a few years now. But we hesitate to use Mathilde. We've never needed anyone before.

After thinking about it for a few days, we finally decide to pay her, if only to see what she can offer. Once we've recovered completely, we make our way back to the vacant lot, knowing she'll come to find us there. The first visit yields nothing. Mathilde isn't there. The second time, she plants herself in front of us as we're sitting side by side at the foot of the silo.

"You ready?"

We hand her the money in response. There is no more negotiation. Mathilde unrolls the rope and tosses the hooked end toward the ladder. We hadn't noticed the hook the first time. She is clearly accustomed to doing this, seeing as it takes her only three tries to get the hook onto the first metal rung. Holding the rope firmly in one hand and the hammer in the other, she climbs easily up the wall, her feet planted in familiar divots. When she stands up on the ladder, she lets the hammer fall in front of us, inviting us to do the same. It takes considerable effort and we lose our footing several times, but after a few tries, we manage to climb the wall. Getting up the ladder is easy, if dizzying, after our first try.

Mathilde punches the door, which opens with a loud creak. She disappears above us. Once we reach the summit, we finally gain entrance into the cavern.

It takes a moment for our eyes to adjust to the darkness. We slowly begin to make out the interior of the silo.

At first, we can only see the opening. Then we realize that around the border of the walls hangs a large platform that descends in levels inside the depths of the tower. The outside ladder has a matching one inside that allows you to access the pit directly. Large bolts, hoses, and hooks cover the walls. The whole centre is empty, with a twenty-metre drop. The platform is a good metre wide, but we take a step back nonetheless; that chasm wants to eat us up, and there is no railing to hold onto.

We can imagine that at one time, the structure was full of grain. What would happen if we fell in here? Was it dense enough to hold the weight of a person, or would you sink, like in deep water?

We don't know.

Mathilde doesn't share our nervousness. She is sitting down, her feel dangling in the void. We notice a sleeping bag, a canteen, and a Petzl headlamp behind her. Does she really sleep here?

"I've only spent one night here so far. I told my parents I was staying over at a friend's house. But I'm moving in soon," she said.

"You're not afraid you'll fall while you're asleep?"

"I tie the rope around myself and attach it to this hook," she says, pointing to a loop above her.

We try to imagine how a little rope like this could hold her if she fell and doubt the effectiveness of the technique.

"Why do you want to run away?"

It's a personal question. This isn't like us.

"Because I don't need anyone."

We are quiet for a long time. The outside noise is dulled by the silo. The high, sharp pitches that normally harass us are softened here. The world is reduced to this one image of the void, to the structure's metallic smell. We feel at peace here, soothed.

It's warm inside, about thirty degrees. Mathilde is sweating in her long-sleeved shirt. She finally removes it, pulling it over her head by the collar, like a man. Underneath, she's wearing a white tank top. Her breasts are pointy.

We pay her no attention.

"We'll come spend the night here sometimes, too."

We don't ask permission. After all, the silo doesn't belong to her. Now that we know how to get in, we don't need her anymore.

Mathilde shrugs.

On King Street, there's a Mountain Equipment Co-op that sells camping and sports equipment. We've found a use for our allowance. We take the subway there, since we plan to return with bags that will be too heavy for our bikes.

"I'll expect you back before dinner," Emma says, without asking where we're going.

The subway isn't far. By cutting through the school park, we can get there in less than five minutes. There are a number of stops between us and downtown, and we have to change lines halfway. We rarely take the subway. The station smells like dust and bleached urine. The train isn't very full and we easily find seats next to a window.

The stations go by in silence. They're all different, each one distinctly decorated.

The train stops at one station and takes a while to start again. A mother struggles to roll on her heavily loaded stroller. She has to try a few times and finally succeeds by backing on. The doors finally close again.

"It was that one."

"Yes. I remember the staircase."

"It's been almost ten years..."

We blink slowly, our teeth clenched, making our jaw muscles protrude. The train starts back up and we turn to look back at the station disappearing behind us.

On the tiles covering the walls, a mosaic spells "Museum."

The sporting goods store is three storeys, with a climbing wall dominating the centre. We stroll through the aisles. Canteens, flashlights, plastic dishes, dehydrated food, knives... we want everything.

"How much do we have?"

"Two hundred and ten dollars."

The merchandise is not only on display, you can try it out, or at least some items, on the interior climbing wall. A man is on the wall, testing climbing shoes.

We quickly find the rope and hammers. We have to ask a clerk for help using them. It's hard. Numerous climbing ropes are on rolls, sold by the metre. The tools, however, are locked behind a glass cabinet. There are no prices listed for these items.

This will be more complicated than we had thought.

"Can I help you?" A girl in a MEC T-shirt stops beside us.

"We need a hammer and a rope."

"A hammer? You mean a pick?"

We don't like her smile.

"What kind of climbing is it for?"

We were going to answer that it was for climbing a wall, but weren't sure that was precise enough.

"A concrete surface."

"Concrete? These picks are for ice."

We don't respond. A moment passes and the salesgirl continues.

"I'd suggest this one then," she says, indicating a complicated pick, curved on both ends.

Then she sells us nine metres of professional climbing rope.

"We also need a knife, like a hunting knife."

"How old are you?" she asks, skeptical.

How old do you have to be to buy a hunting knife? We can't exaggerate the lie or we'll look ridiculous.

"Sixteen."

"You have to be at least eighteen," she declares.

We'll remember that.

The two items cost everything we have. We'll have to forget about the other things we'd chosen.

The pick and the rope are too precious to leave in the vacant lot. We decide to hide them under the bed in our swim bag. That way we can carry it around without Emma asking what's in it; she'll believe we're still going to the pool. To make sure she doesn't find anything, we wrap everything up in our towels and bury them in the bottom of the bag, with our bathing suits on top. The bag is stuffed full, but if we force it a little, we can still get the zipper done up.

We spend the next week working on throwing the rope, which we've attached to a hook we found in Emma's garden shed.

"That's some pro gear you've got there," teases Mathilde as she arrives.

Her appearances don't surprise us anymore. We make sure to come to the silo when no one is around, but Mathilde's presence, unlike that of others, makes no difference to us. She watches us hook the rope onto one of the ladder rungs. We climb halfway up, then stop for an instant and throw her the pick. She looks up and smiles at us, but we've already turned back to continue climbing.

We take up our position from last time. Evening is just falling and it's cool out.

"Are you going to stay the night?" Mathilde asks, noticing our sleeping bags.

We had brought the sleeping bags a few days earlier, as well as two strong ropes that we'd found at the Grace Street house to protect us from a fall into the depths. But we hadn't yet spent a night in the silo.

"Yes."

"I'm staying too."

Mathilde imposes her presence as evidence. There is nothing else to say and the day stretches into night.

When no more light penetrates the rusted holes, Mathilde lights her head lamp. We brought camping flashlights. She gets completely undressed and stuffs her clothes into her bag.

Seeing her naked body gives us an erection and we start masturbating to make it go away. Her hands behind her head, Mathilde watches us working ourselves in the lamplight. Our breathing is amplified by the echo.

"Do you want me to do it?" she asks.

We say nothing, watching her approach. She jerks us off. Her breasts bounce in rhythm with her hand. Her ass, amazingly round considering her thinness, hovers close to the edge. She straddles us to keep from falling. Her vagina is completely hairless and the way she kneels opens it gently against our legs. Her clitoris pokes out between her pink lips. We want to plunge our fingers into the soft flesh. We only touch the outside before we ejaculate. Mathilde licks up the semen spread out on our stomach and goes to bed.

We wipe up the rest with our sleeping bag. It smells of stuffed toys.

AS I PASSED THE TWINS' ROOM, I was surprised to find the door open. It was still early and it was rare they were up this early on a Saturday morning. I entered cautiously. The beds were messy, but empty. Had they gotten up while I was in the shower?

After a brief tour of the house, I realized they weren't there. The night before, we'd had dinner together, and they'd gone back to their room while I watched a movie on Netflix. I went to bed early. Had their bedroom door been closed then? I thought it had. Had they gone out after that? Had they slept here? Slowly putting together the situation, I began to panic, worrying they'd had some kind of accident. I called Gregory immediately, forgetting he was in British Columbia, where it was still nighttime.

"The twins aren't home—I don't know where they are! I don't even know whether they slept at home. I tried calling them, but they're not answering, as usual." I was in tears.

Gregory was sound asleep on the other end of the line and struggled to understand what I was telling him.

"Emma, listen, calm down. They're almost sixteen. It was Friday night. They've probably been out partying and will be home soon. You just have to explain to them that it's important they tell you where they are if they don't spend the night at home, that's all."

"But they never go out at night—"

"Emma, it's okay if they go out with friends. That's what we want."

"That's what we want?" I sniffled, trying to calm down.

"I'm tired, Emma. It's five in the morning here. Wait a few more hours, and if they haven't come home by noon, call me. Otherwise, text me and tell me where they were, okay? I'm sure it'll be fine. Stop worrying. And don't punish them when they come home. It's important that they have friends."

I made myself a coffee and sat on the couch, scanning the sidewalk from the window for their return. A stream of people walked their dogs past, but I didn't see the twins. I waited for a long time, and was going to make myself a second cappuccino when at last the front door opened.

"Finally! Where were you?"

They were puffy-eyed, rumpled, and dishevelled. They had obviously been out partying all night. It took them a moment before they decided to answer.

"We were with friends."

I took a long inhale. "Were you drinking?"

"No." They crinkled their noses as though I'd said something absurd.

"It's important that you tell me if you're not coming home to sleep. I was so worried. I need to know where you're spending the night. I would have called the police if Daddy hadn't reasoned with me."

They looked at me like they hadn't understood a word.

SCHOOL STARTED BACK UP. All our classes were boring, except for technology. Our teacher, Ariel, lets us call him by his first name. It's his first year teaching. He is taller than us. His face is covered by a powerful beard, which blends in with his bushy hair. Gregory also has a beard, but his is grey. They don't look anything alike. Ariel's voice is deep and calm, and his words seem to flow like liquid. We have tried to imitate him, but no matter how we try, we can't get it right. Our voice is sharp, with ridiculous accents. We've always hated it.

Technology is the only class we have together. Our other classes are at different times, but we can see each other at lunch. We sit together in the cafeteria. One day, Mathilde comes and sits at our table. We didn't know she went to our school. Behind us, people whisper.

"I haven't seen you at the silo lately."

She puts her tray down in front of us.

"I have something else to show you if you want."

We meet up with her after school.

We follow her, walking our bikes, since she's on foot. On the way, she stops to say hi to several friends. It's annoying.

We end up in a dirty alleyway covered in graffiti, where the College Street restaurants keep their garbage bins. There's as much garbage on the ground as in the receptacles.

The stink of piss and vomit is suffocating. Filth sticks to the wheels of our bikes and leaves a muddy trail behind them.

Mathilde stops in front of a metal door with no handle and knocks. The door opens onto a steep staircase. We follow her and the boy in the apron before her. They lead us into a dark room that acts as storage for the restaurant we've just entered through the service door.

A series of metal shelves holds rows of cardboard boxes, sacks of rice, and white dishware. The worker nods at Mathilde and leaves. Nothing in the room interests us.

"It's twenty dollars for a blowjob," says Mathilde.

We raise our eyebrows and cross our arms. Pay for that? When we can manage perfectly fine on our own?

"Hurry up, we don't have much time. Who goes first?"

Well, since we're here...

"THE LADY NEXT DOOR SAYS THE BOYS ROBBED HER."

Gregory had just stepped in the door, but I had to tell him right away.

"She's completely paranoid. She says they're going into her house in the middle of the night."

I threw this information at him before he could even respond. He stood in the front hall, his arms loaded with polystyrene containers, and ended up going around me to get to the kitchen and put down the takeout dishes.

"She's lost her mind is all," he said, hoping to end the discussion.

"No kidding. What if she calls the police?"

I was in a panic and Gregory didn't seem to understand why. To him, I was completely overreacting.

"Where are the boys, anyway?" he asked.

"They're not home yet. They should be along any minute." I calmed down a bit.

We had decided we wouldn't monitor their comings and goings, despite Vanya's accident and their night away from home. We were hoping to teach them some responsibility by maintaining certain rules, like eating dinner as a family. In Gregory's opinion, this was the best way to educate the boys and retain their trust. Too much control and we might alienate them and give them reason to lie. I tried to stick to these principles, but it was hard sometimes.

"You have to talk to her."

"To who?" he asked.

Honestly, he wasn't listening. The boys were being treated like criminals and he hadn't even reacted.

"Do you think they could have done it?" he asked, irritated.

"No."

"So, why are you afraid of the police?"

The boys finally came home, looking sleepy. I could have confronted them, but I knew they wouldn't answer my questions. Something in them still resisted.

They had grown up a lot over the summer. They looked like two young men now, and they looked less and less alike as they got older. It was now easy to tell them apart, to the extent that people who didn't know them couldn't guess they were twins. Their facial features were now distinctive; everything about Vanya was hard and sharp, while Daniil was more delicate. They were the same size and body type, but their movements were unique and their gaits easily distinguishable.

"You have your last appointment at the hospital tomorrow, Vanya. You haven't forgotten, have you?"

I put my hand on his arm and felt the muscle tense beneath my fingers. I lifted my hand and turned to Daniil.

"Do you want to come with us?"

Daniil refused. Vanya turned suddenly toward him with a questioning look, but said nothing. I observed their silent exchange. They clearly understood each other without speaking. Shouldn't I be able to as well? Some time ago, it had become clear to me that my sons didn't love me. Even as babies, they hadn't needed me to console or reassure them. They were enough for each other.

The visit to the hospital gave me a chance to talk with Vanya. I picked him up from Harbord College at the appointed hour and let him settle into the car before gently initiating the conversation.

"Did you have a good day? What class did you have this morning? Swimming?" I said, looking at the gym bag he carried.

"No. Tech."

"Ah. And what did you do?"

"Some design."

"Design? Like Daddy?"

"No."

"Did you know I was a designer too, before?"

"Yes, I know."

The discussion dragged. I realized I had no idea what his interests were.

"Do you know what old Aïda told me? She thinks there are robbers going into her house while she's asleep—she's losing her mind, poor thing."

It was obvious that I was testing him. Vanya shifted a little in his seat. A moment passed before he spoke.

"Yes, Aïda's losing her mind," he said, turning suddenly toward me.

He looked me straight in the eye. I could only hold his gaze for a few seconds. He kept looking at me for another moment before turning away. There was nothing else I could add. I drove in silence to SickKids. We didn't say another word as we waited for the consultation.

"How's my friend Vanya?" cried the doctor.

Vanya made a disgusted face and said nothing. The doctor didn't seem to be waiting for an answer, anyway. He was already putting on the sleeve to test Vanya's blood pressure.

"We've got a real athlete here," he continued in the same tone as he put away his gear.

He filled in the file as he examined Vanya's wound. Everything was healing well. He seemed pleased.

"We're just going to finish with a little blood test to make sure there's no anemia."

He handed Vanya a form that he needed to bring to the lab. Vanya nonchalantly handed me the paper. I thanked the doctor on his behalf, and we left.

As we passed the door, I glanced at the form. My son's name appeared at the top. The doctor had checked the test he needed from the list and indicated his blood type: AB-.

It had to be a mistake. Vanya was O+, like his brother. I told Vanya we had to go back, but the doctor had already started a new consultation, and the secretary said he wouldn't be able to see us before the end of the day. Neither my protestations nor my anger would change her mind. Extremely annoyed, I sent Vanya to get his blood taken, and stood outside the examination room, determined to intercept the doctor between appointments. The door soon opened and I was able to ambush him.

"He's O+, not AB-. There's a mistake on the form." I spat the words in his face. The doctor couldn't understand my aggression.

"There's no question about it. We established his blood type in a previous analysis, when he was staying in the hospital," he said.

"But that's impossible. His blood type was written on his medical file when we adopted him." My lip started to tremble.

"There might have been a mistake on their form. It happens sometimes."

He pushed gently past me and continued on his way. I froze for a moment in the hall. Pinned up haphazardly on the white walls around me were posters for cervical cancer screening, domestic violence, alcohol consumption during pregnancy, childhood asthma. I glanced distractedly at them before joining Vanya, who must have finished his test.

"How did it go?"

I looked at the cotton stuck to the inside of his elbow. He looked pale. I moved to touch his cheek, but he turned away violently. I wanted to get home as fast as possible, to check the information in the adoption folder and pay no more attention to his mood.

The folder was in one of the organizers in the filing cabinet that contained our marriage documents, tax information, and various receipts and warrantees accumulated over the years. My organization was impeccable, I could proudly say. I instantly found what I was looking for.

These folders hadn't been opened in more than fifteen years. The boys' baby photos were stapled to the top corner of each page. The medical file was a succinct sheet on which were written the dates of birth and vaccinations, a few notes on the boys' motor development, and the results of a number of blood tests confirming that neither of the boys had HIV or tuberculosis, and finally the blood type: O+.

I called Gregory's cell, even though he hated it when I bothered him at work. He was in New York for meetings.

"You realize this means there could be other mistakes in the file. Their blood type is pretty important, isn't it? If they got that wrong, maybe they were wrong about other things."

Gregory quickly moved to end the call. I should have known long ago that the information wasn't reliable, he told me angrily.

"What if they have AIDS?"

"Emma, I'm busy. Make an appointment with the doctor if you're so worried."

So that's what I did as soon as I hung up.

"SHE SAID NO."

"How much did you offer her?"

"I didn't have time to talk about money. She got mad and said she wasn't a whore."

We're in the dog park, as agreed. We'd caught Mathilde after school to suggest a price to fuck us, and we'd been stunned by her refusal. We thought the only problem might be the cost. Since we bought the climbing material, our funds have been scant. But we're managing. We have ideas.

We say nothing more, but stretch out together and stare into the void. We don't notice the boy with the poodle playing a few metres away. He sees us right away and directs his dog toward us.

He sits down without asking, then throws a ball down the hill to get rid of the dog.

"What are you doing?"

"We're trying to sleep with a girl."

"Oh. Where's the girl?"

"That's the problem. She doesn't want to."

He sits, thinking for an instant. We pay him no attention. It annoys us that he's there.

"My dog tries to mount other bitches too. A lot of times they don't let him."

We turn toward him. The dog has returned with his toy, breathless, tongue hanging out.

"Who's the girl?" he asks.

"You don't know her. She's in high school."

"I know some high school girls," he insists. "I have an older brother. What's her name?"

"You have a brother?"

"Yes. What's her name?"

"Mathilde."

"Don't know her."

It's hard to believe he has a brother; we've never seen them together.

"Does your brother sleep with girls?"

"I don't know. We don't really talk—at least not about that."

"How can you not know? You don't know what your brother does?"

"Well, no. We don't really get along. He never lets me go into his room and doesn't want to play with me."

"You don't do anything together?"

"Sometimes we watch movies."

We don't really understand what he's talking about. He has a brother, but he doesn't know anything about him? We're starting to think he's lying to make himself more interesting.

"If you have a brother, prove it."

"Okay, I'll introduce you. Where do you live?"

"The red door on Grace Street."

"Okay." He skips away with his dog.

"Do you believe him?"

"I don't know. He's weird."

"Are we going to follow him?"

We get right up and start following the boy, keeping a safe distance so he doesn't see us. From Harbord Street, he starts up Shaw. The street is lined with trees, so it's easy to hide. We give him a head start, since we can see him from far away; the street goes straight all the way to Bloor. He soon enters a fenced garden on the right. We wait a moment, then go up the street to his house. The house is semi-detached, like the one on Grace Street, but looks darker because a big tree is growing in front of the main window. There are flowers growing in front of the house and there's a swing on the porch with a pillow that has "DREAM" written on it. Upstairs, there are two gabled windows. One of them might be his room.

The sound of sirens comes from further down Harbord Street. A number of fire trucks go by, followed by ambulances. We're afraid the noise might make the boy or his parents come out and we quickly walk away.

I STARED AT THE SCREEN, nervously wringing my hands. It was on every station: they'd found the remains of little Faye. The Toronto police chief and an RCMP inspector were giving a press conference. Images filmed live at the investigation site told the story.

A city worker had made the discovery while inspecting the silo, which was slated for imminent destruction. Her body had been right under our noses for all these years. The vacant lot was unrecognizable on television. The fire department had opened up a big part of the surface during the search, transforming it into a giant crater.

The silo had a double floor, explained a reporter in high heels. Across from her, the worker stammered, very shaken. The basement was about six feet high. The centre of the reservoir ended in a large funnel, originally used to extract grain.

The employee had been expected to provide a brief report, mainly as an administrative formality, since the fate of the tower, declared dangerous by the city council, was unequivocal. When he'd opened the trap, the stench of decomposing flesh and ammonia had been unbearable.

In the basement cabin, the dry air had mummified the body. A number of common household tools—hammer, pruning shears, hunting knife—had been used to mutilate the child.

The camera zoomed in on the worker's red face.

THE NEXT DAY, I had to bring the boys to the doctor for a checkup. I told myself I would talk to the doctor about the horrible news. Perhaps he could counsel me on how best to tell them that the body of their childhood classmate had been discovered. I really didn't know how to tell them she'd been murdered.

Our family doctor hadn't seen the boys in many years and found them much changed. They had filled right out.

"They look to be in good shape," he said conclusively.

I mentioned the possibility of mistakes in the medical file, and we agreed they would undergo additional testing. He assured me that a few blood tests would suffice.

"Are you sure they don't need X-rays?"

"There's no sense in repeating the tests," he said, as though I was being frivolous. "However," he added, "it wouldn't hurt to talk a little about sexual education."

My eyes widened. I pursed my lips. The doctor handed the boys a few condoms, giving them a few instructions for use. "And remember, it's important to wear a condom for vaginal and anal penetration, and even for oral penetration."

I thought I would die. What kind of ideas was this idiot putting into my children's heads? The twins put the condoms in their pockets and the doctor released them with a lab requisition.

"Let's get out of here," I said, hissing with spite.

Several tubes of blood were taken from each of them. The nurses took no precautions, since they were dealing with such sturdy boys. Standing up from the donation chairs, the boys and the insides of their elbows were the same colour as the chairs. I'd completely forgotten to ask the doctor about Faye.

TODAY, WE DECIDED TO GO FOR A RUN near our school. We don't jog very often, but we wanted to start slow since our fall at the silo. Running requires different breath control than swimming or weight training. Our ankles soften on the steep terrain, but it takes considerable effort.

It's not a forest, but rather a sparse, ill-maintained wood. Broken branches and ferns litter the ground, as well as abandoned beer bottles. At one point, we get winded and have to rest. We sit down on the ground, looking at the grey sky through the canopy of trees.

"Do you think we're sick?"

"No, why?"

"I don't know. All these tests they're making us take..."

"I'm sure it's normal. It must be like the vaccinations we got when we were little."

We hadn't asked Emma the reason for the tests.

"Do you think they can find our real mother with these blood tests?"

We distinctly remember the moment when Emma and Gregory told us they weren't our real parents. Much earlier, Emma had explained reproduction to us, and how the baby grows inside the mother's stomach. We got very scared. Touching Emma disgusts us. Her skin, her mouth, and her hair make our skin crawl, so the idea that we had developed stuck to the surfaces of her body really repulsed us.

As for the fact of having exited through her slimy vagina, it seemed unimaginable. We couldn't sleep for several nights afterwards. In order to come to terms with the idea, we started going into her room to watch her sleep. The room was always warm and smelled harsh, acrid. Emma sleeps on the left and Gregory on the right, when he's there; when he's not there, Emma still sleeps on her half, without touching the other side. Gregory generally sleeps with his back to Emma. She sleeps on her stomach, with her mouth open. Naked. Always. Before, she was smooth, but now her body is fat and soft, with creases like she's melting. Her skin is covered in bumps and craters.

We made up a game: we bring our face right up to Emma's and we breathe in the smell from her mouth, her hair. It makes us want to throw up, but we have to resist. Whoever can stay there the longest wins.

It was such a relief to learn that we hadn't grown inside her stomach. We would rather believe we had never been inside anyone's stomach. That was preferable.

"Come on, let's go," we say.

We run, paying no attention to the roads we take. At the end of a dirt lane, we find ourselves in a cul-de-sac. A building that looks like a big metal container sits at the end of the school's west wing. This is Ariel's office.

Through the window, we can see him working. We watch for a long time, holding our breath. Hes moving gypsum panels. His movements are precise, assured. The effort makes the muscles in his arms and neck bulge. He moves between the work benches as though accomplishing a sports routine.

We knock on the corrugated tin door.

Ariel doesn't seem surprised. We don't return his smile. We ask him if we can come and work in the shop at night. He agrees. He says we can come whenever we want after school, we just have to let him know in advance to make sure he's free.

"I'd ask you not to let our agreement get around, though," he says, "since I can't offer it to the others."

We shake hands and leave.

Built more than a century ago, Harbord Collegiate has a number of concrete buildings. The architecture looks like an underground parking garage, but for a few rectangular windows that let in a minimum of light. They have bars on them to prevent suicide attempts, or that's what they tell us anyway. On the archway over the main doors the motto of the school is engraved in Latin: *Gratia et sapientia proficere.* We don't know what it means.

Sitting on the low wall bordering the entrance, Mathilde watches us walk up the school steps. We look at her coldly. We don't pay attention to her for long; we have an appointment with Ariel today.

The workshop is small, but Ariel has used the space well. In the middle of the room is a big work table with a varnished wood surface that sits atop a metal chest of drawers for storing screws, nails, nuts, electrical wires. Everything is labelled and well organized. When we arrive, Ariel is looking at something on his phone. He puts it down when we walk in.

"Ah—there you are. I was waiting for you."

He closes the door behind us and steps into his office, just off the shop. He returns with two leather belts. We can't believe our eyes.

"Presents!"

He has the same one around his waist, with a number of loops and pockets to hold tools. We put them on right away and start filling them. Ariel believes we have real engineering skill. He gives us a lot of encouragement when we work together. Today, he suggests we help him build some shelves for his tools and manuals.

Ariel treats us like colleagues. We talk about plans and construction, and he listens to our suggestions.

"You'll need to put an extra brace in the middle of the shelf. It'll bend if you put anything heavy on it."

"Right, of course. Thanks."

He lets us work in silence. The smell of wood and glue stays in our hair for a few days. We like going to the workshop. We leave, still wearing our tool belts.

Breathlessly, Emma announces that we have visitors. The boy with the poodle is there, on Grace Street, with a teenage boy we don't know. The boy looks us over. We're wearing a white T-shirt with arrows on the front. The fabric is thin at the shoulders and our collarbones protrude beneath it. The boy doesn't answer the questions we ask him. He seems lost in his thoughts. We have to repeat ourselves:

"What are you doing here? Who is he?"

"This is my brother, Cory."

It's hard to believe. The boy is blond and plump, while the other one has olive skin and the beginnings of a mustache. But they have the same blue eyes, it's true. We move to close the door, but the boy blocks it with his hand.

"What are you doing? You wanted to meet my brother."

"No. We never said that."

The brother makes a weird face that shows one of his canines. "Dude, who are these freaks?"

He turns to go back down the steps. The boy catches him by the elbow.

"Relax, Cory. I told you, I have something to show you."

"This thing better be worth it, Hendrick."

His name is Hendrick, then.

"Come on," he says.

We don't want to follow them. But he insists.

The brother complains as we walk, hands in his pockets.

"Where do you guys know each other from?"

"We don't know each other," we say.

Cory rolls his eyes and turns to Hendrick.

"We swim together sometimes. They're supergood divers!"

Cory seems impressed.

"Why are you wearing carpentry belts?" asks Hendrick, walking around us.

"To do carpentry."

We walk down Crawford Street, not knowing where Hendrick is taking us. Cory walks in front of us lazily. We have to keep slowing down so as not to run into him. Hendrick, for his part, skips along the sidewalk and can't stop talking.

"You should see them dive, Cory—they can jump from a handstand. And they can do all kinds of tricks."

Cory's eyebrows form a *V*. We realize Hendrick is bringing us to the vacant lot. When we finally arrive, we notice the police tape all around the silo. A giant crater has been dug. We turn to Hendrick.

"What happened?"

Cory says, "What? You don't know? Are you from Mars or what? Everyone's talking about it. They found the body of that little girl that was murdered, hidden in the silo!"

We lean in to see where the body was, but since it's dusk, we can't make out the bottom of the hole. Cory looks at the time on his phone.

"What did you want to show us, Hendrick?" he says, giving him a shove.

The boy digs around the outside of the hole and pulls out a rusty knife.

"What's that?" asks Cory.

We understand. "It's the murder weapon. Where did you find it?"

"There," he says, pointing vaguely to a spot in the hole. "But I hid it here so no one finds it."

"You went down there?" Cory cries, disgusted.

Hendrick nods.

"How did the police not find it?" we ask.

Hendrick doesn't know what to say.

"It might be nothing—it might just be an old gardening tool." Cory pushes his brother as he speaks. Hendrick takes a step back.

Standing in front of the hole, we start to get bored.

"What are you doing tonight?" asks Cory, turning toward us. "One of my friends is having a party, if you want to come."

"We don't go to parties."

"Man, what's wrong with you?"

"They don't go out with middle-schoolers..." Mathilde emerges from the woods.

"What do you think you're doing?" Cory asks angrily.

We let them argue for a moment. Mathilde holds a hand out in front of her and says sharply, "You don't go to our school, that's all. Vanya, are you coming?" She smiles.

We cross our arms and wait for her to continue, but she doesn't seem to have anything else to say. She finishes by adding, "Fine, you can bring your brother, if you have to."

We pat our pockets and lift our chin as we walk away together, leaving Hendrick and Cory behind us. We can hear them fighting even once we've turned the corner.

Mathilde makes a quick phone call and drags us back down the service alley of the Chinese restaurant. A man is sitting amid the garbage bags. He has a long beard and dirty hair and he's drinking a beer from a bag, muttering words we don't understand.

A girl opens the door this time. She's wearing a net on her head to keep her hair in place. She greets Mathilde briefly, holding the door for her. She has to hold it with her whole arm because it's heavy. Mathilde enters first. A greasy piece of garbage sticks to our shoe. Holding the door with one hand, we rub our foot along the ground to dislodge the garbage from our sole, but we lose hold of the heavy door and it closes. We stand in the stinking alley. We knock violently several times, calling "Vanya!" No one opens. We wear ourselves out for a while on the door, then give up. The homeless man yells something; we ignore him and leave, shoulders slumped.

In the little room, Mathilde is waiting.

"What do you want?" she asks.

"I want to fuck you."

"I already told Daniil that I don't do that. I'm a virgin. Where is your brother, anyway?"

"I don't know."

"Maybe he changed his mind. So what do you want?"

"Same as last time, I guess."

We pretend to reach for the money in our pocket, but she stops us by nodding her head. "It's okay this time."

Mathilde's ass and legs are soft and supple in our hands. Her muscles aren't as hard as a boy's. We take off our shirt and jeans and stand in front of her for a moment in our underwear. Our erection makes a lump right in front of us. Mathilde looks us over. She spends a long time caressing the scars that stripe our forearms.

"Did you cut yourself, Vanya?" she asks.

We don't respond. Mathilde gets undressed. She's not wearing a bra. She pulls down her cotton panties; an elastic thread sewn in a zigzag makes a kind of lace. The skin of her vagina is firm and seems to have a complicated texture inside. We touch the wet folds. Beneath our fingers, the walls seem both too loose and too tight. If we put a little pressure on it, the flesh sinks in. We don't know how far we can go without hurting her. We pull out our wet fingers and let her take us in her mouth. By keeping our eyes open, we manage to last longer than the time before. Staring at the metal shelves helps to distract us from our pleasure. She doesn't swallow the semen, using her panties to wipe it up before putting them back on. As the fabric dries, it will get crunchy. We know.

"You don't say anything when you come."

We don't understand what she means. We put on our jeans and tell her we have to leave.

"Daniil!"

We had nearly reached the house on Grace Street, angry at finding ourselves alone in that disgusting alleyway. Mathilde repulses us. The boy comes out from the shadows just as we were about to go into the backyard. He smiles with his big teeth.

"It was her, then. Mathilde, eh? So did you manage to sleep with her?" asks Hendrick.

We don't feel like explaining to him what happened. We open the gate, but the boy keeps trotting after us.

"I can sleep with you," he declares.

We turn, cross our arms, and look at him. Hendrick just stands there, but he's shaking a little. His hair has fallen in his eyes. He has a little nose, a big mouth, a skinny neck.

"Okay. Come on."

We get out the bike and point to the seat. The little boy, his eyes lit with joy, takes his place behind us. We pedal standing up.

We head in the direction of the dog park and take the boy toward the woods. As we ride, Hendrick hangs onto our waist to keep his balance. Our abdominal muscles flex beneath his fingers with each push of the pedals. Our body is lithe. Hendrick closes his eyes to fully experience the embrace. The bike speeds on. The wind caresses his face and makes his hair blow back. He presses his cheek against our powerful back.

We lean the bike against a tree and signal with our head. We walk with our hands in our pockets. When we get to the thickest part of the woods, we stop.

"Do you know how to fuck?"

Hendrick lifts his eyes, nodding. He pulls down his pants and underwear, finding himself suddenly half naked in the cool of the little woods. We look distractedly at him, undoing our belt buckle and digging in our pockets.

Hendrick doesn't cry out. He waits, holding onto his tree, until it's over. We come quickly and Hendrick is released. When our hands let go of his hips, he falls to his knees. His eyes fill with tears.

We pull up our pants in silence.

Hendrick is sitting on his hip, like a girl, so as not to put any pressure on his ass. The condom filled with semen lays on the ground beside him. We offer to take him back on the bike. He refuses, but asks, "Does this mean we're friends now?"

We shrug.

RESTING ON MY RIGHT HIP, I held my buttocks apart with my left hand to allow the esthetician to finish my bikini wax. The chemical smell of the green wax on the double boiler stressed me out before she had even begun. Stretched out on the narrow table, my body started to sweat in anticipation of the pain. It only took a few minutes to complete a Brazilian, but it felt like torture.

The treatment room was small and square, the fake leather table taking up most of the space. Lise, my aesthetician, had finished. She told me to take my time, and left. I was sitting on the table with my hands gripping the edge. I could feel the blood pulsing in my wrists. I looked down at my bare feet, and the big blue veins protruding from my white skin. Something trembled slowly inside me. Staring at nothing, I contemplated the void of my thoughts. I had had enough. Of everything.

My Burberry hung behind the door, the fabric sadly worn at the collar. I slid from the table and tackled getting dressed.

The girl at the reception desk wore a bun on top of her head and tattoos on both forearms. She was chummy, despite our obvious age difference. She stamped my loyalty card as I slid Lise's tip into an envelope.

"You're Vanya's mother, right?" she asked, handing back my card.

I nodded.

"We go to the same college. He's a friend of mine... well, really, he's going out with my friend Mathilde," she clarified.

I walked out of the clinic in a daze, my handbag dangling from my shoulder. Vanya had a girlfriend. So he was capable of connecting with people other than his brother. I had no time to pursue this train of thought. I raised a hand to hail a taxi. I was due at our doctor's office in less than a half hour; I had to pick up the twins' blood test results.

"Where are the boys?" asked the doctor, less jovial than usual.

An acidic smell hung in the room, a mix of cleaning products and sweat. I was going to respond that I didn't know, but told him instead they were at school. *With their girlfriend*, I thought to myself, trying to get used to the idea.

"At their age, it's better if I can speak directly with them."

For a moment, I was worried he wouldn't tell me the results, and considering his mood, I feared the worst. After a time, he slowly opened the two folders in front of him and cleared his throat. I hung in rapt anticipation. As I waited for him to deliver the verdict, I crossed and uncrossed my legs. When I shifted in my chair, I could feel my freshly waxed skin against the fabric of my panties.

"We have, at your request, performed a number of tests... which reveal that Daniil and Vanya are in perfect health."

"They don't have AIDS?" I collapsed back against the chair.

"No HIV, no hepatitis, no tuberculosis," he confirmed.

I sighed with joy. They weren't sick.

He paused. "And I can assure you of their blood types. As I told you, Vanya is AB-."

A huge weight lifted from my shoulders. I listened to him, grinning like an idiot. The tests had put my worst fears to rest. I'd been so worried, I'd even started researching new AIDS treatments online. He continued, "And it looks as though Daniil is O+."

None of that mattered anymore. My biggest worry was that one mistake in the adoption file could have been hiding others. I didn't care that they weren't the same blood type, so long as they weren't sick. I thanked him enthusiastically as I picked up my things. I couldn't wait to get out of the office to call Gregory.

The doctor said nothing else, but as he returned my enthusiastic handshake, he looked at me strangely, his eyes wide. I ran my tongue over my teeth, to make sure I didn't have anything stuck in them, and left, thanking him a last time.

Gregory was in Toronto for the month. It was strange to phone him and know he was in the same city.

"Everything is fine. There's nothing wrong with them!"

"Well, perfect, then."

I could hear him eating on the other end of the line. He was on his lunch break.

"Do you have time to meet for a coffee? Could we meet on Queen Street? Just a quick half hour?"

"Hmm... We could meet at Dufflet, but no more than half an hour, okay? I have to lead a meeting at three."

It was always hard convincing him to leave the office. When he was in Toronto, he filled his days to make sure he could get home early and have a little family time. But I needed to see him. This blood test business had really shaken me, and I wanted to celebrate.

We met at the bakery shortly after. Gregory let me have the banquette and took the chair himself. I ordered a tea and a cupcake, and Gregory had an espresso. The aroma of cake was everywhere; I had it in my mouth and lungs at the same time. All my pores seemed full of it.

"So. They're not sick. This is such a relief. I feel so light, you can't even imagine."

"All the same, it would have been surprising to learn anything else. We know they're healthy, they've never even been sick. Not a single childhood illness, nothing. In fifteen years, we'd have seen symptoms. You can't hide tuberculosis for long," he said, teasing. "Anyway, the important thing is that you're relieved."

I rolled my eyes and changed the subject. "How was your morning?"

Phone in hand, he responded evasively. I hadn't paid close attention to his work in a long time. Nearly half the staff at the firm now were people I didn't know. I found out about Gregory's work through his publications, but I didn't know anything about his daily life. We mostly talked about the children when we were together. I smoothed my hair nervously.

"You know what I found out..." I let my sentence hang, trying to create some suspense, but he said nothing. "Vanya has a girlfriend."

"Oh yeah? That's a good thing. He's almost sixteen, it's about time."

I didn't agree. I still thought they were too young to be having relationships.

"I wonder what Daniil thinks of that..."

I was thinking aloud. Gregory raised his eyebrows.

"That's true, it could be a problem for him. He might feel left out."

"Do you think we should do something?"

"Emma, what are you saying? We're not about to start meddling in their relationships."

I wondered if he meant the relationship between them, or with others. It seemed to me we had very little involvement in theirs... too little, perhaps.

Two female students sat at the table next to us, one wearing glasses with frames too big for her narrow face, and the other wearing high-waisted pants. I remembered wearing that very look in the eighties.

I rested my head on my hand, looking at Gregory, trying to remember what he looked like when we first started dating. I wasn't as young as the twins, but nonetheless… it was so long ago. At the time, he wore T-shirts and faded jeans, and he had round, tinted glasses. His hair was much longer and formed a curly ball around his face. Now he gelled his hair back. He took less care of his appearance when he was a student. Now, the bathroom was lined with pomades, oils, and soaps. I think he owned more beauty products that me. Having said that, it worked for him. He had remained a handsome man, and had developed an elegance with age that he hadn't had when he was young.

As soon as my plate was empty, Gregory tilted his head back to catch the last drop of his coffee and got up to pay.

I put on my old trench coat and left without waiting.

The rest of the week was a complete bore. Friday, I did a little shopping for dinner, some cleaning, then I lounged around with a cup of tea. I got out the photo albums, something I often did when I was feeling nostalgic. I turned the pages absently. The first ones were filled with snapshots of the twins when they were just little, then, as their round faces grew narrower, the photos became landscapes, and eventually the twins simply walked out of the frame. It had been a long time since the boys would let anyone take their picture. Gregory didn't appear in a single shot.

My magnificent sons, whom I had never gotten to—or known how to—touch, kiss, comfort. My vision clouded with tears. The photo albums immortalized their childhood, a time when anything was still possible. Maybe, I thought, if I tried even harder, one day or another, I would succeed. It had to work.

I had been patient, had given them time to get to know us, to situate themselves. Perhaps we had waited too long. Perhaps, instead, we should have been harder on them. Gregory believed he had done his best. He was the father he would have wanted to have: understanding, permissive, easygoing.

I stopped at the photos we had taken when we were camping in Muskoka when the twins were still babies. They were sitting on a big rock, looking into the camera, almost smiling. Their faces were in focus and the woods were blurred behind them. Their resemblance didn't seem so striking all of a sudden. With my head tilted, I was studying each of their features when the ringing of my phone interrupted my thoughts and made me jump. When I had to confirm that I was the mother of Daniil and Vanya, I knew that something serious had happened.

The college management asked that we come and meet with the disciplinary committee. Immediately.

After my urgent call, Gregory dropped everything and met me in a panic on the front steps of the college.

"What happened?" he asked, out of breath.

"I don't know. They said there was an incident, but I don't know what. They're not hurt. That's all I know."

The assistant who met us wouldn't answer a single question, no matter how we insisted. Instead, she locked us away in a boardroom with an oval table taking up the whole space. The room smelled like dark wood and mildew.

"What do you think could have happened?" I asked Gregory, needing to break the silence.

"I don't know. Maybe they got in a fight."

Gregory was tapping his fingers on the table, agitatedly looking at the time on his phone, which locked and unlocked in irritating clicks. I scanned every corner of the room, but there was nothing to look at.

Just then, the door opened and a bunch of people, ten or so, came in and sat down. At the end was a woman I felt I knew, a brunette with an aquiline nose.

The principal cleared his throat and tapped his pencil on a stack of sheets in front of him.

"Okay. TDSB protocol requires that I introduce all the parties. So, for the sake of the minutes—you're getting this, Mrs. Cruz?—we have: Bronwyn Patel, history and math teacher, John Von, information technology teacher, and Ariel Brunswick, technology teacher, who, along with me, make up the disciplinary committee of the college, along with Charles and Bridget Vince, the plaintiffs, and finally Gregory and Emma Dominik, parents of Daniil and Vanya. There. No sense in tiptoeing around. Mr. and Mrs. Vince have told us about a very troubling relationship between their youngest son, Hendrick, ten years old, student at Montrose Junior Public School, and yours, Daniil and Vanya, fifteen years old, students here at Harbord Collegiate Institute. They met with Hendrick a number of times at the pool, supposedly to teach him to dive. Note that they would have shared dressing rooms. Daniil and Vanya, furthermore, followed him home. Bridget here witnessed them loitering near the house. And Thursday, September 28, after school, around five-thirty, Daniil took Hendrick into the woods and raped him. Then he abandoned Hendrick, alone and wounded."

I cocked my head. He had spoken quickly and had a thickly accented English. I wasn't sure I'd caught it all.

"Has the act been confirmed by a medical exam?"

Gregory's voice made me jump. He was very determined and self-assured. I glanced toward the principal, waiting for his answer.

"No."

"No, there was no medical exam, or no, there hasn't been a confirmation?"

Gregory's tone was poised and professional. I didn't understand where he was going with his questions. My head was pounding. I placed a hand on my forehead. My fingers were like ice.

"The medical exam didn't confirm the penetration," the principal responded, imposing his gaze on Gregory.

Bridget stood up, her chair screeching against the floor. "Hendrick waited three weeks before telling us. The exam couldn't have been conclusive."

"Come on! A child who's been sodomized, excuse me, but there are going to be signs," Gregory spluttered.

I recognized her right away; she was a neighbour I saw often. She lived close, on Crawford Street, or Roxton, maybe. The young technology teacher had been looking at me since the beginning of the interview. Around the oval table, he was sitting right across from me. He looked barely older than the twins. He looked extremely sad.

"Emma, did your sons say anything to you?" asked the principal.

Hearing my name, I lifted my eyebrows and gave him a flat smile.

"They didn't say anything to me."

I got out my hand cream to calm myself. I looked at the parking lot through the window. It was afternoon and the students had begun filtering out from the campus.

"Listen, what are we doing here, exactly?" continued Gregory. "We're talking about the word of kids who aren't even here. And what's your authority to deal with this issue? It has nothing to do with the college, from what I can understand."

As he spoke, Gregory scanned the room. The father, who had kept his arms crossed up to that point, laid his hands on the table.

"Hendrick gave us details that a ten-year-old boy couldn't have known. He's a shy, reserved boy. He admired your sons and they took advantage of him."

A violent cramp made me double over in my seat, but no one was paying attention to me. I let it pass, closing my eyes to hide the pain.

"My boys are shy and reserved too!" shouted Gregory. "Maybe they had a misunderstanding."

"A misunderstanding? Your son raped Hendrick by mistake, is that it?"

The mother's face was purple and distorted by her tears. The father had put his arm around her shoulders, but she shrugged him sharply off.

"Mrs. Cruz, please disregard that last interjection," said the principal. "Listen, let's stay calm, this is a very difficult situation for everyone—"

"Are you making a formal complaint?" Gregory cut in. "Because if so, I'll alert my lawyer and we can continue this conversation in an official context. But I'm starting to understand. You know that this will go nowhere with the police, because there's no proof, isn't that right?"

"We are here to establish what happened," the principal continued, though his assurance was crumbling before Gregory's determination.

"Without the involved parties present?" snapped Gregory sarcastically. "Without us having the chance to talk to our sons? You make us come here, with only one side of the story established, deliberately keeping us in the dark. I'm going to tell you what this is: it's profiling. You've already decided that our sons are guilty, because they're different. Because they don't fit in like the others, and doesn't that just make them the perfect suspects? Well, I won't allow it. Is there a formal complaint? No. So nothing is keeping us here. Excuse me, but I have things to do. Emma, come on."

I stood up without fully unfolding my body, and walked out stooped, without looking back. Gregory strode briskly down the hallway lined with metal lockers.

"Unbelievable. What do they think? We're going to let them say whatever they want about the boys, just because they don't fit the mould? They don't know who they're dealing with. I have to get on a plane to Dallas in less than an hour, and they're going to make me miss my flight on top of it all. I don't want you to mention this to the twins while I'm gone. I'll deal with it when I get home."

I stopped trying to follow in his footsteps; he was too fast. With my arms dangling at my sides, I weaved home.

I WOKE UP DRENCHED IN SWEAT, BREATHLESS. I tried to inhale deeply, but something blocked it. I couldn't seem to get any air. What was going on?

One hand on my chest, I started panting in shallow breaths, but it wasn't enough. I looked around me to try and find help. The room was empty and the house silent.

I was alone. I was dying.

Around me, the walls started to swim, the slats of the blinds hypnotizing me. I was going to faint. I had to get hold of myself. Was I having a heart attack? I closed my eyes and tried to focus to calm down, but I couldn't. I had to get help.

I got some breath and tried to call "Gregory," but no sound came out. I couldn't remember whether he was home or away. I didn't know whether the boys were there either. My lips moved in the emptiness, trying to form the names of the twins, without success.

My clothes stuck to my stomach, suffocating me. I pulled my collar until a ripping sound released me. I took a long inhalation and felt air filling the depths of my throat. I drank several gulps of air until at last I came back to life. I was breathing. I hiccupped like a child after a sobbing fit, still shaken with panicked spasms. I fell back into the pillows, spent.

I stayed that way, stretched out, helpless. Of my ripped T-shirt, only the collar and a great, gaping hole remained on my damp chest. I closed my eyes and plunged back into sleep.

I woke up in the same position. When I lifted my eyes, I saw them. They were looking at me, side by side in the doorway. I couldn't hold back a cry. I rolled myself up in the covers to hide my naked body.

"What are you doing there?"

"We heard you scream."

I looked at one of them, then the other. I didn't believe them, with the way they leered.

"It's fine. I'm fine. Go away."

Vanya shrugged and they both turned in one gesture, disappearing from my sight. I didn't understand what had happened. Was it an angina attack, a stroke? I should probably get myself to the doctor to check, but I felt better. There remained only an almost-imperceptible tremor inside me. I waited a bit before getting up, playing it safe.

I carefully set my feet on the floor, testing my strength. I seemed fine. *A shower will put me right*, I thought.

I washed my hair, exfoliated my face, and shaved my armpits and legs. I wiped the steam from the hand mirror and got out all my kits.

First, I applied a flawless base coat, mixing a little BB cream with my moisturizer. With the concealer brush, I hid the wrinkles around my eyes and a little redness around my nose. I devoted considerable time to applying the perfect smoky eye with a gold eyeshadow and a nice, thick mascara, and finished with a Bordeaux lipstick and matching blush. Then I put my hair in a twist and went to get dressed. I let my movements guide me, one leading to the other without my intervention. The spontaneity was intoxicating. I felt good. In the walk-in closet, I picked out a form-fitting cocktail dress. It had gotten too tight, but I still managed to close the zipper over my stomach.

The twins were in the kitchen. I know they watched me leave, but I paid them no attention. I just grabbed my Vuitton and went.

I was leaving. I didn't know where, but I was leaving.

I started the car, intending to go as far as I could. I drove down streets and turned corners with no goal or specific destination. I wasn't going anywhere; I was leaving. It was the leaving that was important, not the arriving. The car did as I asked—it went forward, that's all I wanted. At a red light, I had to stop, which felt counterintuitive. I pulled a little on my dress, which was climbing up my thighs, and floored the accelerator.

On the Gardiner, the traffic was moving smoothly. I made the Don Valley Parkway in a few minutes, and merged onto the 401 without thinking. I hadn't turned on the radio. I was just listening to the roar of the engine, the noise of the highway, the silence in my head. I paid attention to all my blind spots, signalling clearly, keeping my hands in perfect position on the wheel, my back straight. This was enough for me. I didn't feel capable of more. I drove, refusing to think about the state in which I'd woken up that morning. I drove, forbidding myself to think about the boys standing in the doorway. I drove, avoiding the question of why I was running away. I was the road, the fleeting buildings, the disappearing trees. I was motion. I didn't look back.

The 401 went on forever. I sped past cities and towns without crossing them, without ever touching down. Ontario could have been Italy, Japan, or Texas—everything seemed so smooth now.

I don't know when I exited the 401 for Highway 49, but I have to believe I did, since I found myself on Main Street in

Picton, where, after countless hours of uninterrupted driving, I had to stop. There was a little fork in the road, and I went right, parked, and got out at a bookstore-café.

In my cocktail dress, I had a chai latte in Picton. I spent a long time looking at the cinnamon floating atop the milk foam, my fingers trembling gently against the flowered cup. Outside, it was grey and a few raindrops splattered against the front window. I sighed and took a long drink of the sweet tea. I hadn't eaten anything all day and I thought I could feel the liquid travelling through me like a mood. I woke up enough to check the time. It was a quarter to five in the afternoon. I had reached no conclusions.

I got up without finishing my tea and walked into the bookstore. I knew Picton. I'd been here at least twice with Gregory. When we moved to Toronto, everyone was talking about Prince Edward County, for its vineyards, its cheese-makers, its beaches. We followed the recommendations and rented a pretty little cottage close to everything. We sampled the local wines, went swimming at Sandbanks, looked for a good deal at the antique shops in the area. Those were beautiful moments, it seemed to me, but thinking about it now, nothing stood out. I didn't remember anything in particular about those vacations, other than the feeling of a time upon which we had turned the page.

I wandered around the bookstore, not looking at anything; there was nothing I wanted to buy. My glance fell on the Alice Munro books display next to the cash. I was already heading for the exit when I noticed a pile of newspapers.

There was a picture of the twins on the front page.

The investigation into Faye's murder had suddenly progressed and they were actively looking for two individuals. New interviews had revealed the presence of two suspicious men on the site of the discovery. Witnesses described them as two tall blond men. It was an artist's rendering on the cover, but they were so real, I almost thought it was a photo. There was no doubt whatsoever: the composite artist had drawn my sons.

My knees suddenly started to shake. I understood. Faye. Fe. Their tattoos—they were for her.

Something rose up in me, a cry, a howl, a long, anguished wail, suppressed for fifteen years. I grabbed my phone with a sure hand and dialed the number of the hotline. In a series of incoherent sobs, I recited my life story—the stillborn baby, the twins' adoption, their withdrawal, their silence, their isolation, their tattoos, the rape. Everything.

TWO POLICE OFFICERS PUSH US FORCEFULLY toward the vehicle parked across the entrance. We don't resist, we let them. The neighbours are excited by the flashing lights. With their arms crossed or hands over their mouths, increasing in numbers outside the Grace Street house. When we pass in front of them, they shout insults at us, their words overlapping, indistinct.

In the doorway, Gregory stands rigidly in his suit. He'd come home last night. His suitcase is still in the front hall. A police officer is watching the front steps, stopping the media from climbing up to ambush Gregory. A TV camera sweeps over the crowd, with a reporter interviewing the people standing in a line on the lawn belonging to a neighbour, who watches through the curtains.

We are not handcuffed, but the officers hold us firmly by the arm to direct us: their hold makes us lower our shoulders. They throw us down on the seat. The force of their gestures takes us way back, to something buried deep in us. Our bodies remember. The hands that assault us bring a memory trembling to the surface. Touch that hurts; we remember it well.

Everyone is pointing at us.

That's when we see Mathilde, her hood covering her head and a heavy bag on her back, among the crowd watching our arrest. With a shrug, she hikes up the strap of her bag and walks away, her pretty face turned toward the ground.

The police car starts suddenly, fending off the mob that refuses to disperse. No one explains to us what is happening. Whatever happens, we will tell them nothing.

I TOOK MY TIME TO COME HOME, shower, and change my clothes. The house was empty. Gregory had left that morning to be with the twins. They were being held at 14 Division. I took off all my makeup, tied my hair back with an elastic, and put on a pair of silk pants and a tunic. I was drained. I hadn't slept and had driven all night, stopping for coffee, getting stuck in traffic jams on the way into Toronto. I should have taken a nap, but they had already been waiting hours for me. I begrudgingly climbed back in the car.

At the police station, they made me identify myself several times before bringing me into a dark room. Blinded by the fluorescent lights in the hallway, it took a moment for my eyes to adjust to the darkness. Gregory was sitting on a stool, and didn't turn when I walked in. A jacketed officer stood beside him, detailing what was happening on the other side of the window. The wall facing us was the back side of a one-way mirror through which you could see the twins being interrogated, one after the other, in the adjoining room.

Vanya was being questioned when I arrived. The interrogation must have been going on for some time, because he looked demolished. His face was sunken. Something in his features had collapsed.

"You have her name tattooed on your feet. Why?"

"Everyone forgot. We didn't want to forget."

"So you admit it."

"We got a tattoo of her name."

"Was it your idea or your brother's to kidnap Faye?"

"We didn't kidnap her."

"You killed her, you hid her in Museum Station, and then you moved her remains into the silo. How did you transport her all that distance?"

"We didn't transport her all that way."

"Did you carry her on your bikes? In a cart?"

"No."

"You were six years old. Did you have an accomplice?"

"We didn't kill her."

"It's in your best interests to confess, if you want to save your brother."

On hearing these words, Vanya flipped the table over onto the interrogating officer.

"My brother didn't do anything."

He then turned violently toward us and punched the mirror. The glass didn't break, but was marked with a long streak of blood. His hand swelled right up, but Vanya didn't seem to notice the pain.

"Get him out of here. Go get me the other one," bellowed the officer, coming out from behind the table.

It was an endless day. We waited for hours in the grey hallways, drinking weak coffee. Gregory stood rigidly at my side. We hadn't said a word to each other. There was nothing left to say. His presence to me seemed secondary, useless.

Finally, they brought us into the inspector's office. The sickening smell of stale tobacco filled the room.

"We interrogated them for over five hours. They didn't crack."

"But you do think they did it, right?" I shot back.

"Like I say, they haven't admitted anything. We've searched their phones. They're completely empty. That's a little strange. Do they have another one?"

"Not that I know of."

"We even performed the DNA tests you suggested to the Belleville police."

Gregory stood up suddenly.

"She did what?" he stammered.

"Calm down and sit down right now, sir."

Gregory sat back down.

"When she gave her deposition in Belleville, your wife suggested that we take DNA samples from your sons. But it turned up nothing. They don't match the results from the investigation. We have nothing against them. You've put me in a terrible position with the press. Now I'm going to have to backtrack on this whole story... Once again, we're going to look like idiots. This investigation is a nightmare."

He was thinking aloud, chewing on a toothpick. He didn't look at us, only at the papers tacked to the wall. The office was a dusty mess. He took the toothpick out of his mouth and turned to us.

"You've wasted my time. This story makes no sense. They were barely six years old at the time. Whoever mutilated Faye had physical strength, experience in dissecting a body, and a level of perversion impossible in a child. They needed cold patience and time to massacre a little girl like this. Your boys are the kind of damaged kids I've seen hundreds of, but they're not criminals."

What did he know? Did he really know them so well after a few hours of questioning? Was he the one who tried to raise them? To love them?

"Has Vanya been treated for his self-mutilation?"

The shock made me jump backwards. My chin started to tremble. Gregory closed his eyes and clenched his fists on the arms of the chair, hating me with all his being.

"You didn't see anything, I suppose? Is that it?" The inspector nodded as he spoke, looking at us with disdain. "Fucking rich boys. They're worse than the rest of them." He chewed his words. I wasn't sure I understood.

"And what about the rape?" I asked.

"It's just not clear, that one. There's no proof, and the boy's account is inconsistent. I don't think they've got enough for a charge. They might ask that your boys be sent to reform school, I don't know. I didn't do the follow-up." He was quiet for a moment. "All right, I've had enough of you. Get out of my office and go get your boys. They're in booth six."

We got up, and Gregory headed straight for the door. The room was tiny, and he had to turn sideways to keep from touching me. The torn leather of the chair had been scratching my legs that whole time, but I only noticed it at that moment. I rubbed my thighs to get rid of the marks.

I didn't recognize the men they returned to me. The twins seemed to have suddenly grown up. The shadow of stubble darkened their faces. We walked one behind the other without speaking, or really looking at each other. I didn't know what to do with them anymore.

The inspector poked his head out the door of his office. "The exit is to the right, there."

He held a folder, which he used to direct us. We didn't react. None of us seemed ready to initiate leaving. The inspector stepped out into the hall, arms crossed, vigorously chewing gum. "By the way... the DNA tests you requested... your sons? They're not twins. They're not even brothers."

He spoke without moving toward us, spitting his words. He kept talking about blood types and genetic connection, and I thought I could see the words bouncing off the walls of the corridor like rubber balls. I didn't see the man anymore. He was just a little shadow in the distance. I followed the movement of the balls, watching to see if they would reach me.

We left the station.

Gregory drove. I don't remember the journey, only the arrival. As we pulled into the driveway, we were jolted for a second. Gregory had missed the corner and climbed the embankment.

He got out of the car, his lips white, and kicked the tire before reaching a hand out for the hood to get his balance. He staggered into the house and crumpled into the armchair in the living room.

The boys stood in the front hall, speechless and slack, lost in our home. I saw them as babies again, finding their place for the first time in this space. They'd never settled into this house. They had never even stepped over the threshold.

I saw them only from a distance as they simultaneously turned toward each other, gazing in silence for a long moment. It was the muffled thud of the first punch that made me react. Vanya and Daniil clutched each other by the shoulders and were brutally fighting each other. Daniil's nose was already broken, and Vanya's lip was bloodied. Their entwined bodies contorted with the violence of the blows. Gregory approached to try and separate them, but his efforts didn't even shake them. He got an elbow to the chin, which threw him back, staggering.

The tiles of the entranceway were slick with bloody spittle, in which the boys slid until a shot to the temple made

Daniil lose consciousness. Vanya breathlessly continued beating the still body before crawling away.

They weren't brothers anymore.

Gregory approached them cautiously. Daniil came to his senses and tried to stand. Gregory pulled up his rumpled pant leg and sat down with them. He was breathing heavily. He ran a trembling hand through his hair and leaned toward the boys as if to take them into his arms. Moving together, Daniil and Vanya lifted themselves onto all fours and looked at Gregory. Their eyes were little more than narrow slits. They then opened their mouths in inhuman grins and threw themselves on him. Daniil scratched him in the face and Vanya grabbed the arm he'd extended them and twisted it behind his back. Gregory got free, screaming, his arms flailing.

Petrified in the middle of the living room, I couldn't move.

As he escaped, Gregory climbed up a few steps on the staircase. He continued climbing, watching the boys, who sat beneath him, now unmoving. His cheek was striped with deep scratches.

A loud commotion came from upstairs. I ran upstairs toward it, shouting Gregory's name, but I couldn't stop him. He'd lost his mind. He was ransacking their room.

He grabbed one of the beds and turned it on its side to get it through the door, bowling me over in the doorway. Brandishing it, he flew effortlessly down the stairs, opened the door to the porch, and threw out the bed, which shattered into pieces. I dropped to my knees at the top of the stairs, following his movements with my head, both hands covering my mouth, my face dripping with tears.

Pushing the boys aside with his foot, Gregory stomped back up the stairs. He went to grab one of their desks, then suddenly stopped cold, looking at the space left by the bed. I dragged myself over to him.

The bed had hidden a clutter that was now visible. Releasing the desk, Gregory began breathlessly digging into the mess. When I approached him, he pushed me away with his hand. I backed up, but I stayed.

He pulled Vanya's swimming bag toward him and unzipped it. Hesitantly, he spread out the contents. The items were dirty. When Gregory laid them out, dry, sandy earth fell from everything. There was a long rope, a pick, meat hooks, a hunting knife, a big set of pruning shears, and bundles of money.

And fur. A lot of fur.

With a flick of his wrist, Gregory dumped out the bag, shaking it, and started sobbing. I couldn't see his face, but his back convulsed. I leaned in closer. He held up his hands, black with earth, in front of his face. Between his spread fingers hung tufts of blond hair.

His breathing shifted to a rasping wail. Then, in a gesture of madness, he started rubbing his face with his dirty hands and turned suddenly toward me. Hair stuck to his scratched face, which was wet with tears; his skin was caked with dirt and dark red lumps stuck to his cheeks. He collapsed on the ground shaking his head, psychotic. I ran out, screaming.

THE MAN STANDING IN FRONT OF US had seen this before. So had we. Today, after months of processing, it was coming to an end. I sat very straight on my chair, aware of the rhythm of my breath, slow and deep. Next to me, Gregory coughed. He cleared his throat several times, trying to catch his breath.

The social worker peered blankly at our heavy file. To his left, the string from a teabag dangled from a paper cup. Mechanically, he dunked the bag in a useless gesture, punctuating his speech by taking little sips of the beverage, no doubt cold by now.

The meeting stretched on. I did most of the talking. I had already told our story a number of times, to a number of other counsellors. Over the course of the interviews, the story had become more succinct, and now only the highlights remained, the ones that'd led to our decision. The more times I told it, the more sense it made. The sequence of events was clear. There could be no other conclusion.

On the melamine desk was a row of framed dogs. I scratched a spot on my pants. Gregory had started biting his nails. We kept our eyes to ourselves.

"In general, everything in the adoption folder was false, you say. Look, it happens more often than you think... But the criminal file is brand new, so... Yes, I have a copy here. All right."

The hairs on the back of my neck stood up, setting off a slow shudder that ran down my whole back before settling into my kidneys. I straightened up. My life was a lie. The DNA tests revealed a completely unique set of genetic baggage for each boy. Perfect strangers. The social worker filled in a series of sheets before handing them to us to initial. I'd already given so many signatures, the gesture had become automatic. There was only one pen. I had to share it with Gregory. We passed it without glancing at each other.

Behind us, a printer rumbled without pause as dozens of sheets piled up. Following my eyes, the social worker explained, "You think this is bad; this is nothing. We shortened the forms this year. It was much worse before."

He paused for a moment, seemingly lost in contemplation of his diploma, hanging on the wall. "I see more and more cases like yours—not just for adoptive families."

He took off his glasses and started cleaning them with a handkerchief that matched his bowtie. The glasses were thick. He set them down on our file, which acted as a magnifying glass on one of the paragraphs.

"To be honest, it doesn't much matter to us. From the moment you renounce your parental rights, Daniil and Vanya will be integrated into the system as two unique individuals. In any case, at their age, it's unlikely they'd be placed in the same foster home, brothers or not."

After a brief hesitation, he continued, to himself. "Twins, I don't know... It's different, twins... Don't see that much... Might try to place them together... Well, anyway... Whatever happens, they're not twins."

I listened distractedly. Gregory said nothing. For months now, we'd been in no hurry. He could keep babbling for as long as he wanted, it wouldn't change anything. For us, it was over.

ACKNOWLEDGEMENTS

If there's any merit in this text, it's thanks to Fabienne Claire Caland-Rouby, Melissa Dion-Robichaud, Catherine Larochelle, Mathieu Paradis, Anne Caumartin, Nathalie Spurway, and EL.

If I survived it, it's thanks to Gaspard, Malik, Axel, Colin, and Flore, who don't like stories with unhappy endings.

INVISIBLE PUBLISHING produces fine Canadian literature for those who enjoy such things. As an independent, not-for-profit publisher, our work includes building communities that sustain and encourage engaging, literary, and current writing.

Invisible Publishing has been in operation for over a decade. We released our first fiction titles in the spring of 2007, and our catalogue has come to include works of graphic fiction and non-fiction, pop culture biographies, experimental poetry, and prose.

We are committed to publishing diverse voices and experiences. In acknowledging historical and systemic barriers, and the limits of our existing catalogue, we strongly encourage writers from LGBTQ2SIA+ communities, Indigenous writers, and writers of colour to submit their work.

Invisible Publishing is also home to the Bibliophonic series of music books and the Throwback series of CanLit reissues.

If you'd like to know more, please get in touch: info@invisiblepublishing.com